The Random House
CHILDREN'S TREASURE CHEST

The Random House

CHILDREN'S TREASURE CHEST

CLASSICS FOR CHILDREN

NURSERY RHYMES, BEDTIME STORIES, NONSENSE POEMS AND MUCH MORE

Edited by Alice Mills

GRAMERCY BOOKS
NEW YORK

Contents

လ၆ြာ

လ၆ြာ

Introduction

This collection is packed with treasures from the past that deserve to be remembered, along with familiar favorites in different settings. *The Random House Treasure Chest* holds goodies for all ages of children, from those who are just beginning to recognize numbers, the letters of the alphabet, shapes and colors, to those who can read for themselves; but most of all it is designed to read to a child, for parent and child to share the pleasure of a story and its illustrations together.

There are plenty of nursery rhymes here, with illustrations from long ago. Some are very familiar but many are unfamiliar rhymes that children enjoyed listening to and saying, a hundred years ago and more. A few are brand new nursery rhymes that I wrote especially for this book, for contemporary readers, but still keeping the charming, old-fashioned illustrations. These nursery rhymes and pictures are a lovely way to settle a child into sleep.

So too are the bedtime stories. Here we have included some of the less well known Grimm brothers' fairy tales, making them just long enough to be good read-alouds. We have added to the mix a story about Robert the Bruce and the spider (along with many other parts of his struggle to become King of Scotland). Our choice of stories is full of examples of bravery and perseverance, generosity and kindness. The fairy tales abound in characters who are laughed at or treated badly at the start, but who find a way to earn respect, gain love and a place in the world. Such stories can speak to any child who might experience unhappy times.

There are other stories and poems in this book that speak directly to the child's imagination. There is Lewis Carroll's version of

Alice in Wonderland written especially for very young children. *The Treasure Chest*'s retelling of *Gulliver's Travels* presents one of the most memorable and evocative of all stories, of the man who traveled to islands of wonder. There are some children who have a strong preference for realist stories rather than tales of fantasy and imagination, and we have catered for these children with our short version of the story of Robinson Crusoe on his island, as well as with the tale of Robert the Bruce. *Queen of the Pirate Isle* is an old tale from over a hundred years ago, which has fun with the power of a child's imagination, able to create new characters and play out adventures with a minimum of props—a feather, a broom, and an old sheet.

Children do not even need this amount of material to enter the world of imaginative play. The words of the nursery rhymes and fairy tales are doorways into new worlds, which every child can explore at leisure. The pictures speak of times past, of how people used to live and work and the kind of clothes they used to wear, opening up another kind of doorway into imagining the historical past. What might it have been like to live a century or two ago, like young Lily Sweetbriar? Or eight hundred years ago, when kings led their armies into battle? Or in the days of sailing ships when not every island in the world had been mapped and measured?

There is yet another doorway to imaginative play in our *Treasure Chest*, into the world of nonsense. The nonsense poems we include encourage the child to play with the sounds and meanings of words, and to enjoy the humor of their quirky inventions.

From poems that take just a moment to read aloud, through five-minute bedtime tales to stories that might be read over several nights, *The Random House Children's Treasure Chest* is appropriate for parents reading to their children and for children old enough to read to themselves. There is no better gift for a child than one that encourages their own imagination, enhances their play and feeds their heart with story.

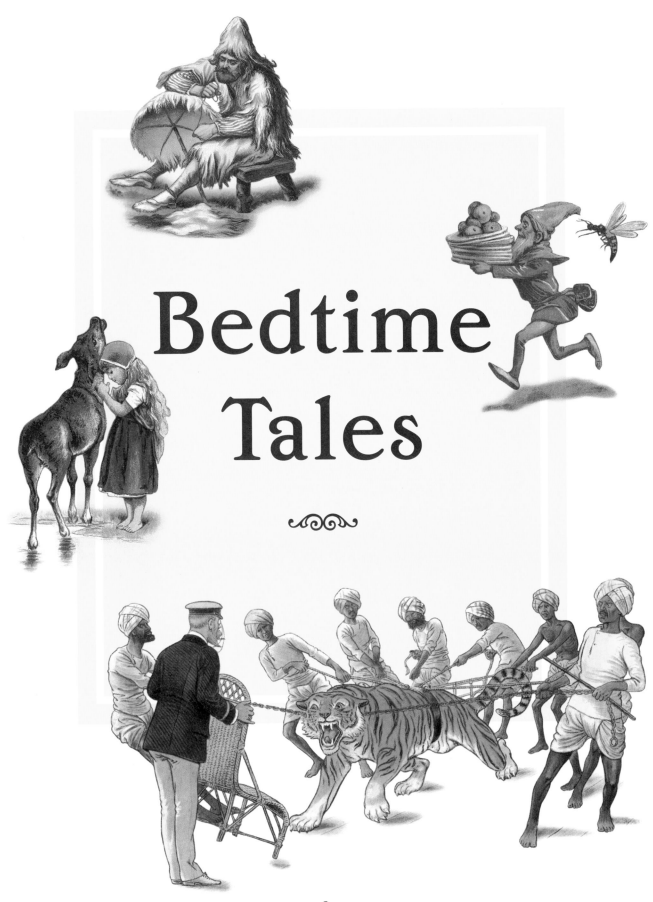

Bedtime
Tales

The Green Fiddler

This is the story of a cheery looking fellow who is often found lying basking in the warm sunshine with his hat drawn down over his eyes. He's called the Fiddler. You may hear him playing on the violin in the summer evenings. Not so very long ago he lived in the country with his good friend Mr Beetle. They had a faithful housekeeper, Miss Moth. She was a rare woman and so clever and sweet. She was a true friend to her masters; she cooked delicious dinners for them; and, while doing her housework, sang the most beautiful songs and was always happy. Their favorite dish was porridge, but when she wanted to spoil them she gave them gingerbread for tea.

Our dear Mr Beetle worked very hard at his digging and Miss Moth often took him a cup of chocolate. Then when the day's work was over the three friends sat down to rest under the shade of a large mushroom. There the Green Fiddler of the Fields played those favorite songs and dances that you all know. Miss Moth really understood music and her heart beat with joy when she heard him play his finest melodies. These three chums had a good time and did not envy the king his castle or the rich man his gold.

One day everybody woke up feeling very happy. Notices had been posted about a ball that was to take place in the Royal Gardens at five o'clock—a real jolly midsummer ball. "Come along," it read, "all who are able to walk and crawl and who have money in their purses. It only costs one straw and everyone is welcome." Tiny little fairies came to the ball dressed in fluffy dresses of different hue. They are the children of the wood and

know how to dance before they can walk. They do not need a dancing teacher like other children. They danced to the lovely music of the Fiddler but Miss Moth enjoyed listening to the lively airs he played and seeing all the fairies so happy.

During an interval in the dancing there was going to be a snail race and everyone was so interested in it that all the tickets were sold out the day before. The Queen of the Butterflies who arrived in a golden coach was to act as the judge. As soon as she gave the

signal the race began and all the spectators watched the very keen struggle of the Snails to get to first place.

"Hop! Hop!" Mr Beetle cried to his favorite, "Don't be so nervous or you'll fall!" Who would think that a snail could rear like that? Snails are always supposed to be slow creatures, but these rushed along the road to the winning post. The first prize was a snail shell of pure gold—the winner would be proud of his victory but no-one wanted to be last as he knew he would be put into the black pot.

Now the ball was ended and the summer days passed quickly away. As the dark days of winter came on Mr Beetle had to work hard crawling into every den and gathering food for his friends until the perspiration was streaming down his back. He always believed in being energetic. "Push and go," and "Do it now," were his mottoes. But alas! One day when he was working so hard he wasn't careful enough. And it all happened so suddenly!

Lumbering along the road came a huge traction engine with heavy wheels. "Creak! Creak!" said the noisy monster; but before Mr Beetle could get out of the way he was knocked over and

killed. Poor Mr Beetle! We felt very sad because we were very fond of him. My dear young readers, you must always be careful when you are walking in the streets or in the woods because accidents may happen to children and grown-ups as well as to beetles.

While the bees flew out to work and returned merrily our good friend was buried under the little hill in the orchard. The Fiddler grieved and grieved until his heart felt very heavy but, as for Miss Moth, she could not be comforted at all. She thought that the world was empty and that everything looked black and desolate. That is the way of the world. Things change quickly as the years go by. Sometimes we laugh and sometimes we cry but we should always make the best of it whether it be good or bad. Are you not all sorry for the Fiddler now—left alone and without friends?

But the birds were flying towards the sky singing with joy. The Fiddler heard their morning songs and roused himself from his grief. He had now no friends to give him food. While they lived he had spent all his time in cultivating his art; now he made up his mind to walk round outside the houses playing the newest waltzes on his violin.

Father Frog didn't appreciate good music and his children preferred the tunes they could jazz to. They danced and jazzed while

14

their eyes were sparkling with joy. They were Peter Croak's three children. Do you remember him? Now he is called Father Frog and he is proud of his three boys.

Well, after the Fiddler played everything they wanted, they sometimes put a penny into his hat. He was always very grateful to them because a penny bought him a good meal, but they often cheated him and gave him buttons instead of pennies.

He was a very industrious musician and his playing made many
people happy. But there are sometimes nasty creatures about who
want to do harm to innocent Fiddlers. One day he got an awful
fright; an ugly fat toad jumped at him and tried to catch him in a
net. It looked like a big goblin with wicked eyes—just the same as
one of those bad creatures you read about in fairy tales. The
Fiddler could hear his enemy smacking his lips at the thought of
fried meatball. But help came to him in his hour of need. Just as
the net was closing over him he heard the flapping of wings and a
strange sound that scared the nasty toad away.

It was the dear little fairies flying towards the shore. They came
down to the ground as soon as they saw what was happening to
the Fiddler. He was lying on the road and looked so pale that they
doubted whether he could get over the terrible fright. They had

not forgotten the days when they danced to his exquisite music. Now was their chance to help him. Their kind hearts knew what to do. They spoke soft and loving words in his ear, raised him up and gave him a cupful of the sweetest flower juice to drink. Then they made a couch of slender twigs for him to rest on and tried to make him smile. When he felt a little better they carried him home to a cosy little bed where he was nursed back to good health and strength. Wasn't it nice that help came to the Green Fiddler when he was having such a hard time?

While the ground was covered with snow and the cold wind was howling outside, the Fiddler was very comfortable in his warm bed and soon recovered under the kind attentions of the

fairies. They felt his pulse every day and gave him all the medicines he required. We hope he always swallowed them nicely! One of them tidied up his room and another read fairy tales out of a big book to him. They gave him chicken soup and porridge with sugar on the top, which he liked very much. Before long he was able to get up out of his bed and three days later he could jump right up to the ceiling.

Hurrah! it is summer again and the Fiddler is cheerful and happy. He plays all the sweet melodies on his violin just as he did in the days gone by. The cheery flowers straighten their backs and open their petals with joy when they hear

18

him. Mrs Sponge is rocking her hat to keep time with the music and Miss Strawberry thinks that the Fiddler is sweeter than honey.

My deal little children, you must feel that the Fiddler has now got over all his difficulties. It was not easy for him but he faced them all bravely and now he has overcome them. So, as the whole tale ends well, do you not feel as happy and contented as the Fiddler is?

Tippoo the Tiger

While he was abroad, Dr Delany, Surgeon on Her Majesty's Troopship *Sarigampis*, read a pathetic appeal from the committee of the Zoological Society of his native city in Ireland, for contributions of any rare bird, beast or reptile. He responded by sending a snake, and received in return a letter of thanks and a printed certificate of Fellowship of the Society.

This little reptile, which wriggles in and out of the story for a moment, was the main cause of the following tales. Keen to earn another certificate from the Society, Dr Delany wrote to a friend asking him to send him anything in the zoological way he might come across on his travels around the world.

In due time Dr Delany was advised that a fine young tiger was on its way to him. "Holy turf! a toiger! I didn't bargain for quite so big a consignment as that."

That night he dreamt of various tigers, captive and otherwise, which he remembered seeing in magazines and books.

After a long wait, "Tippoo" the tiger finally arrived.

During the earlier part of the homeward voyage Tippoo was a great pet with everyone. But towards the end, familiarity, and a lack of respect, caused his popularity to wane. Some people thought that he was "a great nuisance".

Now that the voyage was over, new difficulties arose. Hotelkeepers weren't eager to have the Doctor and his protegé stay in their hotel, and they suggested he try lodgings. Even to get these, the Doctor had to use diplomacy and airily described Tippoo as "a pet, madam, of the cat species"! When, however, the Doctor's luggage arrived, some of it inspired dire forebodings in the gentle heart of his landlady.

Knowing he would soon part with his pet the Doctor had his photograph taken. Tip would sit "as good as gold" while the photographer was getting ready, but the moment his head disappeared under the black cloth, down Tippoo would jump and playfully stalk him. The only way the Doctor could calm him down was to give him a large glass of a soothing syrup. Then Tippoo finally rested!

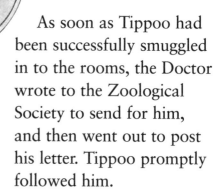

As soon as Tippoo had been successfully smuggled in to the rooms, the Doctor wrote to the Zoological Society to send for him, and then went out to post his letter. Tippoo promptly followed him.

To the Doctor's great dismay, he received the following reply to his letter:

Dear Sir,
I am directed by the committee of the Dundrum Zoological Gardens to thank you for your thoughtful, considerate and public-spirited action in obtaining and offering them a tiger.

They must, however, sorrowfully admit that funds are low—the D.Z.G. being in its infancy—and, as tigers consume so much animal food, and require a special class of attendants, they regretfully decline your exceedingly kind offer.

If you would write again in a few years they would be extremely grateful of the opportunity of reconsidering their decision.

I am, Dear Sir,
Faithfully yours,
Pat Hennessey
Hon. Sec.
P.S. Could you, now, be getting us a bear that would live on bun offerings.

What a blow!

Now, Tippoo was very affectionate—and playful. Especially in the morning.

But matters came to a crisis when Julie, the landlady's daughter, found him sharpening his claws, in the orthodox feline manner, on the legs of the piano. A notice to stop, together with various letters, was pushed under the door.

Tippoo devoured the lot with evident relish.

What's more, Julia subsequently proved to be a ministering angel.

Tippoo was kept in the kitchen, temporarily. It is, perhaps, needless to add that he escaped.

People could barely believe their eyes when they spied Tippoo! He created a great panic in the street!

Dr Delany begged them to reconsider their decision, and, to prove the harmlessness of poor Tippoo, started to play with his whiskers … Julia showed presence of mind—and muscle—and pulled the tiger away from poor Dr Delany.

But there was really no harm in poor Tippoo.

"Come and see my tiger lily," said Mrs de Jonnes to her pastor. "Oh, goodness gracious me!" she cried as she looked over the garden wall, where somehow, Tippoo had become caught up in a tennis net.

The neighborhood was up in arms. "Spare him!"

cried the Doctor, appearing at a window. After much shouting and arguing, the people allowed the Doctor to take poor Tippoo back to his lodgings. He immediately wrote to his friend who agreed that Tippoo did not belong in the city.

So after a wonderful adventure, Tippoo the tiger happily returned to his jungle home.

The Great Fairy Ball

THE PLAYFUL ELVES

Elves	Wake up! Wake up, you sleepy Gnomes! Why don't you wake and play with us?
Gnomes	Be off, you Elves, play by yourselves, We don't want you to stay with us!
Elves	Get up! Get up, you lazy Gnomes! Or really we must tickle you!
Gnomes	You Imps, begone! If you go on, We'll get a rod and pickle you!
Elves	But what are we to do, do, do, If we mayn't bother you, you, you? If you sleep all day and will not play, Pray, what are we to do with you? You'll find without a doubt, doubt, doubt, We mean to rout you out, out, out; If you sleep all day and will not play, We'll turn the kingdom inside out.

IN COUNCIL

1st Gnome	Something must be done, Or else there'll be a riot: Punishment or fun, To keep the people quiet.
2nd Gnome	Let us have a ball, Let us have a supper, Ask the fairy circles all, The lower and the upper; All we will invite, No matter rank or features, Elf and Sprite and woodland wight, And all the forest creatures. And ask their gracious Majesties, The Fairy King and Queen, To grace the ball and festival We'll keep on Golden Green.
1st Gnome	Vote then! Shall we have a supper and a ball?
2nd Gnome	I say yes.
All	And so say we all.

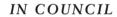

1st Gnome   Now bring the pens and ink and the invitation list,
And be very, very careful that nobody is missed;
And write the invitations in a big round hand,
And send them out and round about,
To all in Elfin Land.

The Ball Committee	Oyez! Oyez! Oyez! Oyez!

The Ball
Committee
  Oyez! Oyez! Oyez! Oyez!
We are the Ball Committee,
The most select and circumspect
Of any in Elfin City.
Now, if any have not been asked,
Let them come for an invitation;
  And though we expect the right to reject,
  We'll attend to each application.
  For if anyone should be missed
  We admit it would be a pity,
  So make no fuss, but apply to us,
  For we are the Ball Committee.
  And if after all you are asked to the ball,
  It is thanks to the Ball Committee,
The most select and circumspect
Of any in Elfin City.

Gnomes
  Hang the Ball Committee!
They are too select;
It would be a pity
Any to reject.
So let's hang the tickets
Here on rock and tree;
All in glade and thickets
Then can plainly see.
Oyez! Oyez! They'll clearly say,
Come to the fairy ball—
Elf and Sprite and woodland wight,
Come ye, one and all!
Come ye all to Golden Green,
For the ball prepare!
For the Fairy King and Queen
Will be there—
—be there!

"How enchanting!" said the Fairies
To the Elf upon the tree.
"I'm invited!"
"I'm delighted!"
Said the Hornets,
"So are we!"
"Oh, how jolly! I'm invited!
Oh, how splendid it will be!"
"I'm invited!"
"I'm delighted!"
Said the Beetles,
"So are we!"

Mouse	Pray, Mister Mole, can you spare me your skin, For my last year's waistcoat isn't fit to go in?
Mole	But if I spare my skin, Sir, what am I to do, For I have been invited to the party too?
Wasp	Pray, Mister Spider, will you measure me? Cobweb, or bat's-wing, which shall it be?
Spider	You shall have the best, Sir, I have upon the shelf, The very latest fashion—I'm going there myself!
Madam Frog	Pray, Madam Silkworm, will you spin for me, For I must have a new dress, as everyone can see?
Madam Silkworm	If you all want silk, Ma'am, what am I to do, For I have been invited to the party too?

Gnome	Come along, Redcap. Come along, Brown; We must go to market, Into Elfin Town.
Gnomes	Good morning, Mistress Sparrow! Have you any fruit?
Mistress Sparrow	Yes, Sir, plenty! Anything to suit. Cherries for the Elf King, apples for the Queen, And pears for the jolly Gnomes, who live on the green.
Gnome	Good morning, Mistress Bee! Have you any honey?
Mistress Bee	Yes, Sir, plenty, if you have the money. Honey for the Elf King, honey for the Queen, And honey for the jolly Gnomes to feast on the green.

THE FAIRY RING

Swing! Swing! Let the scythe swing,
Mowing the grass for the fairy ring;
Cut down the thistles and make it all sweet,
Tender and smooth for the delicate feet!
Mow away, Redcap! Sweep away, Brown!
For the Fairies are coming from Elfin Town;
The Lords and the Ladies, the King and his Queen—
Hie away, fly away, Imps of the green!
Hie away, fly away, bid them make haste,
The night is advancing, there's no time to waste!
The feast, it is ready, lights, music and all,
And we're all of us waiting to dance at the ball.

THE COMING OF THE KING AND QUEEN

The Company Lo! Here they come with fairy band,
King and Queen a-maying;
See how he holds her little hand!
Hark what he's softly saying!

Fairy King We want no stars, my Queen of May,
To show the way we're going;
We need no fairy harps to play,
No horns of Elf Land blowing.
We need no birds to beckon sweet,
No flow'rs our pathway strowing,
For Love himself will guide our feet,
For Love is all our going.

The Company Lo! Here they come with fairy band,
King and Queen a-maying;
See how he holds her little hand!
Hark what he's softly saying!

Beetles Oh, which is the way to the fairy feast,
Kind gentlemen, tell us, pray!

31

Elves	Turn to the south and follow your mouth, And you'll get there one day.
Beetles	But the feast is tonight, we want to be there— We've not had a morsel today.
Elves	Oh, do be content, if on feasting you're bent, Your mouth is the easiest way.

THE UNINVITED GUESTS

"Who stole the spoons? Who was the thief?"
"I," said the Magpie, under the leaf.
"And lackaday me! That must be
The reason no-one has invited me!"
"Who left her house and forgot to return?"
"I," said the Ladybird, "I left it to burn.
And lackaday me! That must be
The reason no-one has invited me!"
"Who drove his neighbor mad all through
    the day?"
  "I," said the Raven, "that is my way.
  And lackaday me! That must be
   The reason no-one has invited me!"
   "Who hooted all the night and
   made people dour?"
  "I," said the Owl, "for I love to be sour.
  And lackaday me! That must be
The reason no-one has invited me!"

32

THE FEAST

Come, sit ye down, the feast is spread,
The cups are ready for the drinking,
While the nightingale sings overhead,
And the merry, merry moon is winking!
And he who will not quaff the bowl,
And set the wine a-flowing,
Sooth, he must be a sorry, sorry soul,
And a wight not worth our knowing.
Here's a health unto their Majesties,
And long may they rule o'er us;
A health to ourselves, merry, merry, Elves,
A health and a rousing chorus!
Come, sit ye down, the feast is spread,
The cups are ready for the drinking,
While the nightingale sings overhead,
And the merry, merry moon is winking!

Elves	Here come the waiters! What shall we do? Trip them, nip them, and slip right through. Ho! Mister Waiters, down you go! Who was it tripped you? Ho! ho! ho! Who was it nipped you—can't you see? Ho! Mister Waiters, you can't catch me!
Master of the Ceremonies	Now let the music play.

Fairy Queen

Dance away, dance away,
Bear me along,
King of my heart,
And lord of my song!
Over the king-cups,
And over the dew—
I only am happy
When dancing with you.

There's a bird in my bosom
That sings night and day—
Love, do you hear it,
Singing for aye?
It is mine, it is yours,
It is loving and true,
For the bird is my heart
That is singing for you!

34

BLINDMAN LOVE

Then out of the woods with a smile so gay,
'Tis Blindman Brownie coming to play;
   "Ha! ha!" cried the Fairies, wild with glee.
      "No, Master Blindman; you shan't catch me!"
       But however they raced and however they ran,
         They couldn't escape from the wee wee man;
And the old Moon smiled through the trees above;
"This wee wee man is the Blindman Love!"
Then Love threw away his mad disguise,
And there he stood with his laughing eyes;
And every fairy fell at his knee:
"Please, Mister Blindman, do catch me!"

THE DANDELION CLOCK

Gnomes Bellman, what's the time o'night?
Bellman, tell us true!

The Bellman Blow the Dandelion Clock,
Puff! puff! pooh!

Elves Bellman, what's the time o'night?
What's the hour it said?

The Bellman Time for all to quit the ball,
Time to go to bed!
To bed! to bed in forest green!
To bed at peep o' sun!

Gnomes Goodbye to Fairy King
and Queen!
Goodbye to everyone!

Fairies Away! away!
'Tis the break of day!
Goodbye to everyone!

THE END OF THE FEAST

Elves and Fairies, feast no more,
Lest surfeit bring you sorrow;
For though tonight your hearts be light,
They mayn't be so tomorrow.
Gnomes and Sprites, go, get ye gone!
This comfort ye may borrow:
    Be wise today, and then ye may
     Begin again tomorrow.
     So pause not so, but rise and go,
     There cannot be a question;
     You can't enjoy a feast, you know,
If you have indigestion.

THE PASSING OF
THE KING AND QUEEN

Fairy Queen   Dearest, the feast is over,
The moonlight bids us home:
Good-night to fairy lover,
Good-night to Elf and Gnome.

Fairy King   Hark to the pipers playing,
Over the hills afar!
Come, love, make no delaying,
Mount we our lily car.

Fairy Queen   The way is long before us,
The night is growing late,
The forest darkens o'er us,
But yonder lies our gate.

Both   No harm shall e'er betide me,
No darkness e'er appal,
While thou art close beside me,
And Love is over all!

Gnomes and   So here we go a-fiddling, fiddling, fiddling,
Fairies   Fairy and Elf and Gnome;
'Tis the break of day,
And we must away,
So here we go a-fiddling home.

Elves and   Here we go a-dancing, dancing, dancing,
Sprites   Fairy and Elf and Gnome,
To tuck our little heads
In our leafy beds,
Here we go a-dancing home.

All   Then here we go a-fiddling, fiddling, fiddling,
Fairy and Elf and Gnome,
We'll meet again tonight,
When the moon shines bright,
But *now* we'll go a-fiddling home.

The Owl   Oh, the dewy Daylight, peeping through the glen,
Looking for a sign of the wee wee men!
Where did she find them? What did they say
As she came a-dancing down the woodland way?
Oh, the dewy Daylight! What did she see
As she stood and watched them 'neath the greenwood tree?
Whitecap, Nightcap, Bluecap, and Red,
Each with his blanket in his own cosy bed.
Oh, the dewy Daylight! What did she hear
As she stood and listened with her pink-white ear?
Snorum! snorum! That's all they said,
Whitecap, Nightcap, Bluecap, and Red!
Hush! Do not wake them! Come, come away!
As they wake by the night, they must sleep by the day.
Hush! Come away!

Puss in Boots

Perrault, *The Blue Fairy Book*

There was a miller who died and left to his three sons his mill, his ass and his cat. The eldest had the mill, the second the ass, and the youngest nothing but the cat.

The poor young fellow was quite comfortless at having been given so poor a lot. "My brothers," said he, "may make their living handsomely enough by joining their stocks together; but, for my part, when I have eaten up my cat, and made myself gloves of his skin, I must die of hunger."

The Cat, who heard all this, but pretended he did not, said to him with a grave and serious air: "Do not trouble yourself, my good master; you have nothing else to do but to give me a bag, and get a pair of boots made for me, that I may scamper through the dirt and the brambles, and you shall see that you have not so bad a bargain of me as you imagine."

The Cat's master did not rely very much upon what he said; he had, however, often seen him play a great many cunning tricks to catch rats and mice; when he used to hang by the heels, or hide himself in the flour, and pretend that he were dead; so that he did not altogether despair that the Cat might help in his miserable condition. When the Cat had what he asked for, he booted himself very gallantly, and, putting his bag about his neck, he held the strings of it in his two fore paws, and went into a warren where there were plenty of rabbits. He put bran and thistle into his bag, and, stretching out at length, as if he were dead, he waited for some young rabbits, not yet acquainted with the deceits of the world, to come and rummage in his bag for what he had put into it.

Scarcely had he lain down than he had what he wanted: a rash and foolish young rabbit jumped right into his bag, and Monsieur Puss, immediately drawing the strings tight, took and killed him without pity. He caught and killed several more rabbits in this way.

and so caught them both. He went and made a present of these to the King, as he had done before. The King received the partridges with great pleasure also.

The Cat continued for two or three months to carry His Majesty, from time to time, game of his master's taking. One day in particular, when he knew for certain that he was to take the air along the riverside, with his daughter, the most beautiful princess in the world, he said to his master: "If you will follow my advice your fortune is made. You have nothing else to do but go and wash yourself in the river, where I shall show you, and leave the rest to me."

The Marquis of Carabas did what the Cat advised him to, without knowing why or wherefore. While he was washing the King passed by, and the Cat began to cry

Proud of his prey, he went with it to the palace, and asked to speak with His Majesty. He was shown upstairs into the King's apartment, and, making a low bow, said to him: "I have brought you, sir, a rabbit of the warren, which my noble Lord, the Master of Carabas [for that was the title which Puss was pleased to give his master] "has commanded me to present to Your Majesty from him."

"Tell your master," said the King, "I thank him, and that he gives me a great deal of pleasure."

Another time he went and hid himself among some wheat, holding his bag open and keeping still; and, when a brace of partridges ran into the bag, he drew the strings,

looks, the King's daughter took a secret inclination to him, and the Marquis of Carabas had no sooner cast two or three respectful and somewhat tender glances but she fell in love with him. The King then invited the Marquis to travel with him and his daughter in his coach. The Cat, quite overjoyed to see his project begin to succeed, marched on ahead, and, meeting with some countrymen who were mowing a meadow, he said to them: "Good people, you who are mowing, if you do not tell the King that the meadow you mow belongs to my Lord Marquis of Carabas, you shall be chopped as small as herbs for the pot."

The King did not fail to ask the mowers who the meadow they were mowing belonged to. "To my Lord Marquis of Carabas," they answered all together, for the Cat's threats had made them terribly afraid.

"You see, sir," said the Marquis, "this is a meadow which never fails to yield a plentiful harvest every year."

The Master Cat, who went on ahead, met with some reapers, and said to them: "Good people, you who are reaping, if you do not tell the King that all this wheat you reap belongs to the Marquis of Carabas, you shall be chopped as small as herbs for the pot."

The King, who passed by a moment later, insisted on knowing who all that wheat which he then saw, belonged to. "To my Lord Marquis of Carabas," replied the reapers, and the King was very well pleased with it, as well as the Marquis. The Master Cat, who went always ahead of the coach, said the same words to all he met, and the

out: "Help! help! My Lord Marquis of Carabas is going to be drowned."

At this noise the King, seeing it was the Cat who had so often brought him such good game, commanded his guards to run immediately to the assistance of his Lordship the Marquis of Carabas. While they were drawing the poor Marquis out of the river, the Cat came up and told the King that, while his master was washing, there came by some rogues, who went off with his clothes, though he had cried out: "Thieves! thieves!" several times, as loud as he could.

This cunning Cat had hidden the clothes under a great stone. The King immediately commanded the officers of his wardrobe to run and fetch one of his best suits for the Lord Marquis of Carabas.

The King was amazingly friendly to him, and as the fine clothes set off his good

King was astonished at the vast estates of my Lord Marquis of Carabas.

Monsieur Puss came at last to a stately castle, the master of which was an ogre, the richest that had ever been known; for all the lands which the King had then gone over belonged to this castle. The Cat, who had taken care to inform himself who this ogre was and what he could do, asked to speak with him, saying he could not pass so near his castle without having the honor of paying his respects to him.

The ogre received him as politely as an ogre could do, and made him sit down.

41

"I have been assured," said the Cat, "that you have the gift of being able to change yourself into all sorts of creatures you have a mind to; you can, for example, transform yourself into a lion, or elephant, and the like."

"That is true," answered the ogre very briskly; "and to convince you, you shall see me now become a lion."

Puss was terrified at the sight of a lion so near him. A little while later, when Puss saw that the ogre had resumed his natural form, he calmed down, and admitted he had been very much frightened.

"I have been also informed," said the Cat, "but I do not know how to believe it, that you have also the power to take on you the shape of the smallest animals; for example, to change yourself into a rat or a mouse; but I must admit to you I take this to be impossible."

"Impossible!" cried the ogre; "you shall see that at once." And at the same time he transformed himself into a mouse, and began to run about the floor. No sooner had Puss seen this than he fell upon him and ate him up.

Meanwhile the King, who saw, as he passed, this fine castle of the ogre's, had a mind to go into it. Puss, who heard the noise of His Majesty's coach running over the drawbridge, ran out, and said to the King: "Your Majesty is welcome to this castle of my Lord Marquis of Carabas."

"What! my Lord Marquis," cried the King, "and does this castle also belong to you? There can be nothing finer than this court and all the stately buildings which surround it; let us go into it, if you please."

The Marquis gave his hand to the Princess, and followed the King, who went first. They passed into a great spacious hall, where they found a magnificent feast laid out, which the ogre had prepared for his friends, who were that very day to visit him, but dared not to enter, knowing the King was there. His Majesty was perfectly charmed with all the good qualities of my Lord Marquis of Carabas, as was his daughter, who had fallen desperately in love with him.

Seeing the vast estate he possessed, the King announced: "It will be owing to yourself only, my Lord Marquis, if you are not my son-in-law."

The Marquis, making several low bows, accepted the honor which His Majesty conferred upon him, and forthwith, that very same day, married the charming Princess.

And so Puss became a great lord, and never ran after mice any more—except for his own amusement.

The Funny Little Fellow

One day a tailor of Casgar was sitting outside his shop at work, when he saw a strange little fellow coming down the street, playing on a tabor, and dancing along in such a funny way that everybody was amused by his antics, and the tailor was so pleased with the good humor of the little man that he took him into his house for supper.

Now it happened that the good-natured tailor's wife had cooked some fish, and while they were at supper eating and laughing and talking, the poor little fellow who was hungry, and ate rather too quickly, swallowed a large bone which stuck in his throat. Both the tailor and his wife were alarmed, and tried everything they could think of to keep him from choking, but it was quite useless, and he sank down dying on the floor.

Now the tailor and his wife knew that if the Sultan's soldiers came round they would be accused of killing the little fellow, so they carried the body to the house of a doctor who lived close by, and left it on the stairs, telling the servant that it was a sick man who wanted treatment. Presently the doctor coming down in a hurry tumbled over the body and rolled it down to the bottom of the stairs. Then he thought he had killed his patient.

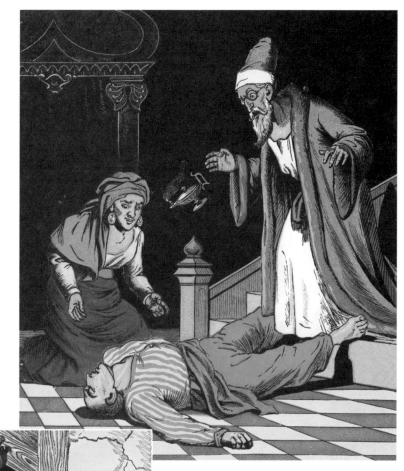

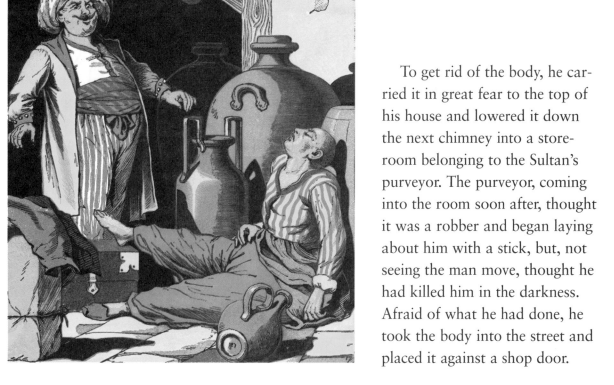

To get rid of the body, he carried it in great fear to the top of his house and lowered it down the next chimney into a storeroom belonging to the Sultan's purveyor. The purveyor, coming into the room soon after, thought it was a robber and began laying about him with a stick, but, not seeing the man move, thought he had killed him in the darkness. Afraid of what he had done, he took the body into the street and placed it against a shop door.

It was a dark street, and a dark night, and presently a merchant on his way home brushed against the body so that it fell from the doorway on its back. Thinking that it was a robber springing on him from behind, he turned round, and while he shouted for help, gave the poor fellow a sound blow with his cudgel, and brought the body to the ground just as the watchmen came round the corner with their lanterns held high.

The watchmen, hearing the cries of the merchant, ran to the spot, and there finding that he had been beating, and as they thought, killing a man, they instantly seized him and bound his hands. The next day they took him before a judge, who at once found him guilty of murder, and sentenced him to be taken outside the city and strangled, with the corpse of the little fellow opposite to him during the execution.

Just as the cord was round the neck of the poor man, there was a shout, and the Sultan's purveyor came running to the spot declaring that *he* had killed the little man. In a moment the cord was off the merchant and round the neck of the purveyor, when a thin man came tearing in out of breath, to say that *he* had done the deed. This was the doctor, and it would have been all over with him, but a third man came panting to say that the man had died in *his* house.

This man was the tailor, who would have been strangled, but at that moment the Sultan came walking by and demanded to be told the whole truth. While he was listening to the story, the doctor was heard to laugh, and presently shouted: "The man's no more dead than I am!" In another minute he put his long thin fingers down the poor man's throat and pulled up the bone. The funny little fellow opened his eyes, stared, sneezed, and recovered.

Robert the Bruce

Retold by Alice Mills

Hundreds of years ago there was a terribly fierce war between the armies of Scotland and England. The leader of the Scottish army was Robert the Bruce, a true nobleman who held the titles of Earl of Carrick and Lord of Annandale.

When Robert was a boy, he lived in the royal court of the English king, Edward I, and the king brought him up to be honorable and truthful, brave and merciful, strong and skilful with his weapons, as a knight should be. While he lived at court, Robert loved England, but as he grew older he started to realize just how badly the English rulers were treating the Scottish people. Although there were many claimants for the Scottish crown, in reality the Scottish people were ruled by Edward, the English king. English soldiers controled every town and castle in the country. They paid no heed to the laws, but seized whatever they wanted without paying for it. If any Scot protested, they paid with their lands, or their money, or even with their very lives.

Robert the Bruce started to plan a war against the English, and he detailed his most secret scheme to another nobleman by the name of Comyn, whom he trusted with his life. But Comyn was loyal to the King of England, not the Scottish lord, and Robert realized that he would have to be killed quickly, to give his war any chance of success. After he had killed Comyn, Robert knew that the English king would take swift revenge, so he decided to claim the crown which was rightfully his (according to his

followers). Of course, the English saw this as wicked rebellion of Edward's subject against his lord. Robert then went on a march to the town of Scone, where the kings of Scotland used to be crowned, and there he claimed the crown of Scotland. King Edward of England had carried off the crown, robes and chair that had traditionally been used for crowning kings. As Robert needed a crown, he took one from a church statue. The bishop lent him some robes and the abbot lent him a chair.

When King Edward discovered that there was now a new king of Scotland, he was full of rage. Although he was old and unwell, he led an army to Scotland, but he could not travel quickly and sent one of his noblemen, the Earl of Pembroke, ahead to begin the attack.

Robert immediately challenged the Earl to single combat in order to decide the war, one knight challenging another so that other soldiers need not die in battle. But it was too late in the day for a formal fight by single combat. The Earl proposed that they should fight the next day, and remain at peace overnight. Robert trusted the Earl's word and led his army into the wood of Methven, where they took off their armour and let their horses start grazing. They were getting their supper ready when, suddenly

and dishonorably, the Earl's army attacked. The Scots were taken by surprise and defeated. The remainder of Robert's army ran away to safety in the mountains of Athole. Robert's queen and his daughter, Princess Marjorie, lived with him in the mountains, and his brother Edward and

Lord James Douglas were his closest allies and friends. Life in the mountains grew very difficult with the approach of winter, so King Robert sent his family to a strong castle, under the protection of his brother Nigel. He took the rest of his loyal men to the little island of Rachlin, four miles off the coast of Ireland, and there they stayed safely through the winter. But Nigel's castle was taken by the English, and the queen and princess were captured.

In the spring, Robert brought his army back to the Scottish island of Arran for a new campaign. First he wanted to retake his castle of Turnberry, now in the hands of the English. He sent a scout to count the English soldiers there, and told the man to light a beacon fire on the hillside above Turnberry, a fire that could be seen from as far away as the isle of Arran.

The scout sailed away and Robert walked to and fro on the beach, anxiously looking out to sea for the signal. At last he spotted a red light far away on the mainland and immediately he set out by boat to attack the castle. But when he arrived, the scout told him that there were so many English soldiers that any attack would be futile. Robert shouted out that he was a traitor, because he had lit the beacon fire when he knew that the Scottish army was so greatly outnumbered. Now the English army would come down to the beach and kill them all.

"You are mistaken, sire," said the scout. "The beacon was already alight when I came here. Someone must have betrayed our plans to the English. I was on my way back to warn you when I saw your boats in the water."

"I for one will not turn back," cried out Prince Edward, and Robert decided to stay on and fight.

That night the Scots won a victory, but afterwards came many defeats. Robert was constantly driven from one hiding place to another, until he felt ready to abandon all hope.

One day he was resting in a cave, hiding from the English, when he noticed a spider hanging from its little thread from the roof. It was trying to swing across to a ledge but again and again it failed. "Will the spider try for a seventh time?" Robert asked himself. "If it gives up or fails, I will give up as well. If it succeeds, I will keep on trying."

Then he watched as the spider tried once more, and this time it reached the ledge. Some say that this tale is only a legend, but perhaps this really was a moment when the fate of kings and kingdoms hung by a spider's thread.

As he kept up the long fight against the English, there were numerous times when Robert was almost taken captive, or even killed. One day the enemy captured his hunting dog and used it to track him down. Robert split up his men into three groups, but the dog knew just

where its master was hiding. It was leading the English closer and closer, and as Robert ran away, he came to a stream in the middle of a wood. He plunged into the water to hide his scent, and splashed away as fast as he could. Fortunately, the dog could not find the scent again, and so Robert managed to escape once more.

Another day, he was with one of his loyal supporters, when they met three men who were carrying swords and axes, who said that they were looking for King Robert, so that they could join his army. Robert was not

certain if these men were loyal to him or spied for the English, and so he did not tell them who he was. They went together to a lonely house where the three men cooked supper and then seemed to fall asleep, but late in the night, Robert woke up to see that they were about to attack. Robert's friend did not survive but the king managed to kill his enemies and escape yet again.

When Robert was trying to evade the bloodhound, he had sent his men away, telling them just where to meet him again. When he came to the meeting place, none of his men were waiting there. He found only the lady of the house, who asked who he was. "A wanderer," said Robert, and

she welcomed him in the name of another special wanderer. "Who is this wanderer?" asked Robert, and she told him, "King Robert the Bruce, and I hope to see him lord and king over all Scotland, in spite of all his enemies."

So then Robert told her who he was, and she brought out her two sons who swore allegiance to the Scottish king. Then up rode Robert's army, with Edward Bruce and Lord James Douglas and one hundred and fifty men.

They fought many battles and started to drive out the English. One castle that they were eager to take from the English was Stirling Castle, and they laid siege to it. The governor of the castle said that he would surrender, if an English army did not come to help him by the middle of the next year. So the English army marched up and confronted the Scottish army, and at the Battle of Bannockburn, the Scots won a mighty victory when the king of England fled from the battlefield. Robert took prisoner some English noblemen at this battle, and he exchanged these prisoners for his wife and daughter, who had been held captive now for eight years in England.

After the Battle of Bannockburn, Robert's army drove the English out of Scotland and began to invade northern England. Now the English were suffering under the thumb of the Scottish army, as the Scots had suffered under their rule before. For twelve years and more, Robert's army harassed the English, until the English king Edward died and his son sought peace between the kingdoms. He gave his sister in marriage to Robert the Bruce's son, David, and recognized Robert as the true king of Scotland.

In the days of Robert the Bruce, leprosy was a common disease in England and Scotland, and Robert fell sick with leprosy. He could no longer rule in a crowded palace, but went to live more quietly by the river Clyde. When he felt well, he liked to organize the building of ships, to add to the Scottish navy, so that his country would be able to defend herself at sea when war came again. He kept a lion in his garden, and loved to hear it roar. He liked to go out hunting with a hawk on his wrist, and now that Scotland was at peace, he even had time for gardening.

When his illness worsened and he knew that he was dying, he asked his noblemen to swear allegiance to his son David, even though the young man was not yet old enough to be king.

Then he asked his friend, Lord James Douglas, to take out his heart after he had died and embalm it. He was to take the heart to the city of Jerusalem. Robert had promised to go on pilgrimage to Jerusalem in thanksgiving for his victories in war and the peace that he had won for Scotland, but now he was not strong enough for the long and arduous journey. Douglas agreed, and Robert said, "Now I shall die in peace, for I know that the best and noblest knight in my kingdom will carry out the promise that I myself can no longer perform."

Then Robert the Bruce died. He was mourned in both castle and cottage, for his might in battle and for his patience and perseverance, in winning the crown of Scotland against the might of the English army. "He compelled even our enemies to respect us," said his people, "and he made the name of Scotland honorable wherever it is heard."

Douglas set off for Jerusalem with a host of other knights and squires. He carried the heart of the dead king in a silver casket, which he hung from his neck. He did not reach Jerusalem, however. Along the way he came upon a battle being fought in Spain against the Saracens and took sides with the Spanish army. Into the battle he led a contingent of the Spanish troops, but the fight went badly for them and he died. The other Scottish noblemen searched for Robert's heart on the battlefield, found it and carried it home again, where it was buried in Melrose Abbey. And this is how Robert's promise was broken without dishonor.

Momotaro

or Little Peachling

A long long time ago there lived an old man and an old woman. One day the old man went to the mountains to cut grass; and the old woman went to the river to wash clothes. While she was washing, a great big thing came tumbling and splashing down the stream. When the old woman saw it she was very glad, and pulled it to her with a piece of bamboo that lay nearby. When she took it up and looked at it she saw that it was a very large peach. She then quickly finished her washing and returned home, intending to give the peach to her old man to eat.

When she cut the peach in two, out came a child from the large kernel. Seeing this, the old couple rejoiced, and named the child Momotaro, or Little Peachling, because he came out of a peach. As both the old people took good care of him, he grew and became strong and enterprizing. So the old couple had their expectations raised, and bestowed even more care on his education.

Momotaro, finding that he excelled everybody in strength, determined to cross over to the island of the devils, take their riches, and come back. He at once consulted with the old man and the old woman about the matter, and got them to make him some dumplings. These he put in his pouch. Besides this he made

every kind of preparation for his journey to the island of the devils and set out.

First a dog came to the side of the way and said; "Momotaro! What have you there hanging at your belt?"

He replied: "I have some of the very best dumplings."

"Give me one and I will go with you," said the dog. So Momotaro took a dumpling out of his pouch and handed it to the dog.

Then a monkey came and got one the same way. A pheasant also came flying and said to him: "Give me a dumpling too, and I will go along with you." So all three went along with him.

In no time at all they arrived at the island of the devils, and at once managed to break through the front gate; Momotaro first, then his three followers. Here they met a great multitude of the devil's retainers who threatened to

fight them, but they pressed still
inwards, and at last encoun-
tered the chief of the devils,
called Akandoji. Then came the
tug of war. Akandoji came at
Momotaro with an iron club,
but Momotaro was ready for
him and dodged him adroitly.

At last they grappled each
other, and without difficulty
Momotaro crushed Akandoji
and tied him with a rope so
tight that he could not even
move. All of this was done in
a fair fight.

After this Akandoji the chief of the devils said he would surrender all his riches. "Out with your riches then," said Momotaro laughing. Having collected and ranged in order a great big pile of precious things, Momotaro took them, and set out for his home. As he marched bravely back he rejoiced that, with the help of his three companions, he had been able so easily to accomplish his goal.

Great was the joy of the old man and the old woman when Momotaro came back. He laid out a beautiful feast for everybody, told many stories of his adventure, displayed his riches, and at last became a leading man, a man of influence, very rich and honorable; a man to be very much congratulated indeed!

Shitakiri Suzume

or The Tongue-cut Sparrow

It is said that once upon a time a cross old woman laid some starch in a basin intending to put it in the clothes in her washtub; but a sparrow that a woman, her neighbor, kept as a pet, ate it up. Seeing this, the cross old woman seized the sparrow, and saying "you hateful thing!", proceeded to cut its tongue. She then let the sparrow go.

When the neighbor woman heard that her pet sparrow had got its tongue cut for this offence, she was greatly grieved, and set out with her husband over the mountains and plains to find where it had gone. As they went they cried out: "Where does the tongue-cut sparrow stay? Where does the tongue-cut sparrow stay?"

At last they found its home. When the sparrow saw that its old master and mistress had come to see it, it rejoiced and brought them into its house and thanked them for their kindness in old times. The sparrow spread a table for them, and loaded it with rice wine and fish till there was no more room, and made its wife and children

and grandchildren all serve the table.

Finally throwing away its drinking cup, it danced a jig called the sparrow's dance. Thus they spent the day.

When it started to grow dark, and they began to talk of going home, the sparrow brought out two wicker baskets and said: "Will you take the heavy one,

or shall I give you the light one?" The old people replied:
"We are old, so give us the light one; it will be easier to carry it."

The sparrow then gave them the light basket and they returned with it to their home. "Let us open it and see what is in it," they said. And when they had opened it and looked they found gold and silver and jewels and rolls of silk. They never expected anything like this. The more they took out the more they found inside. Indeed, the supply was inexhaustible, so that their house at once became rich and prosperous.

When the cross old woman who had cut the sparrow's tongue saw this, she was filled with envy, and went and asked her neighbor where the sparrow lived, and how she could get there. "I will go too," she said, and at once set out on her search.

Again the sparrow brought out two wicker baskets and asked as before: "Will you take the heavy one, or shall I give you the light one?"

Thinking the treasure would be great in proportion to the weight of the basket, the old woman replied: "Let me have the heavy one."

Receiving the basket, she started home with it on her back, the sparrows laughing at her as she went. It was as heavy as a huge stone and hard to carry; but at last she got back with it to her house.

When she took off the lid and looked in, a whole troop of frightful devils came bouncing out from the inside and scared the old woman so much that she ran away and was never heard from again.

The Frog-prince

Grimm, retold by Alice Mills

There was once a king who had a very beautiful daughter. She loved to play at throwing and catching a golden ball, and one day she went into the forest to play. In the forest was a deep stream, and when she threw her ball high into the air and tried to catch it, the ball dropped onto the ground and rolled into the stream.

The princess watched where the ball went, and looked into the water to try to find it, but it had sunk to the bottom and the stream was far too deep for her to see anything there. Then she began to cry and cry, saying, "If only I had my ball again! I would give everything I own to have it back in my hand."

While she was crying like this, someone called out to her, "Whatever is the matter, Princess?"

She looked around to see who could be talking to her, but there was no-one close by except an ugly frog that put its head up out of the water.

"Oh! It's only a horrible frog," she said. "I am crying because my golden ball fell into the water and I cannot get it back."

"Stop crying," croaked the frog. "What will you give me if I bring it back for you?"

"I will give you everything I own—my jewels and my splendid clothes," the princess promised the frog, drying her eyes.

"What good are jewels and splendid clothes to a frog?" croaked the frog. "If you will love me and let me be close to you, sit by you when you are eating, feed me from your golden plate, let me drink from your golden cup, and let me sleep on your bed, if you will promise all this, I will fetch back your golden ball to you."

"Oh, he is such a stupid frog," the young princess thought, "and he thinks so highly of himself, wanting to live in the palace with me. But there is no harm in promising, for he cannot follow me all the way to the castle."

So she promised, and the frog dived down into the water and came up again with the ball in his mouth. He threw it to the princess and she ran off happily. "Wait for me!" the poor frog croaked, but she did not listen. "Wait, Princess, I cannot run as fast as you!" he croaked, but she did not want to hear him. She soon began to play with her golden ball and forgot the frog altogether.

The next day when she was sitting eating dinner with the king and all the court, she heard something hopping and splashing all the way up the stairs, and when it reached the top of the stairs it knocked at the door and called out in a frog's voice, "Princess, open the door!"

She ran to the door and opened it, and there was the frog that she had altogether forgotten about. The princess was frightened and shut the door again, but her father the king said, "Why are you afraid? Is there a monster at the door?"

"No," she said, "it is the ugly frog that lives in the stream, who gave me back my golden ball when it rolled into the water. I promised to let it sit at table with me and eat and drink with me and sleep on my bed, but I never thought that it would come here asking me to open the door for it."

While she was telling this to her father, the frog knocked at the door again and called in his frog's voice, "Princess, open the door!"

The king said to his daughter, "Princess, if you made a promise, then you must keep it. Go and let him in," and the princess went to the door and let the frog come in.

The frog hopped up onto the table close by the princess and croaked, "Princess, let me eat with you, feed me from your golden plate and please let me drink from your golden cup!"

The princess tried to say no, but her father said to her, "Princess, if you made a promise then you must keep it. Give the frog some food from your golden plate, and help him drink from your golden cup."

And so the princess lifted the frog on to the chair beside her, gave him some food from her plate and helped him drink from her cup.

When the frog had eaten and drunk, he croaked, "Princess, I am weary! Take me in your arms and carry me upstairs so I can sleep on your bed!"

The princess wanted to say no, but her father reminded her for the third time that she must keep her promise. So she lifted the cold wet frog into her arms and carried him upstairs to her bed, and there he slept for the whole night.

As soon as it was day the frog hopped away to his stream in the forest, but the next night as the princess was eating her dinner, there came a knocking on the door and there was the frog asking to be let in, to eat from her golden plate and drink from her golden cup and sleep on her bed all night. And the king reminded his daughter that if she made a promise she must keep it, and so the frog came to the table and ate and drank with the princess and slept all night on her bed.

As soon as it was day the frog hopped away, but the next night he came knocking on the door again, to take his place at the table and eat and drink with the princess and sleep on her bed again. In the morning the princess woke up, and the frog was gone. In his place a handsome prince was standing by her bed smiling at her. The prince told her that he had been enchanted by a cruel witch who changed him into the shape of a frog and put a spell on him, so that he could only return to human form if he could find a girl who would let him sit close by her at the table and feed him from her plate and let him drink from her cup, and let him sleep on her bed for three nights. "And so you did, my Princess," he said to her, "and because you were kind to me as a frog I love you dearly as a man. Will you come with me to my kingdom and be my wife?"

And so the spell was broken, and they lived together in complete happiness for the rest of their long lives.

The Tailor's Three Sons

Grimm, retold by Alice Mills

There was once a tailor who had three sons and a goat to give them milk. One day the eldest son was tending the goat, making sure she had plenty to eat, but that night she bleated, "Hungry! Hungry!" The tailor grew angry and told his son to leave home. The same thing happened the next day to the second son, and the next day to the youngest son. The next day the tailor looked after his goat, but again she bleated, "Hungry! Hungry!" when she came home. He punished the goat for lying by shaving her head and driving her away, and he longed for his sons to return home.

The eldest son became apprentice to a furniture maker, and at the end of his apprenticeship his master gave him a little table with magical properties. If anyone said to it, "Prepare for dinner," suddenly it would be laden with wonderful things to eat and drink. The son traveled home with the precious table. Along the way he stayed at an inn and showed the table to the innkeeper, who decided to steal it from

him. In the night, the innkeeper exchanged it for an ordinary table, and when the son came home and said to the table, "Prepare for dinner," he discovered that he had been cheated out of his magical gift.

The second son became apprentice to a miller, and at the end of his apprenticeship his master gave him a donkey with magical properties. If anyone said to the donkey, "Bricklebit," gold pieces would shower out of its mouth. The second son hurried home, but along the way he too was cheated out of his magical gift by the innkeeper.

The third son became apprentice to a turner, and at the end of his apprenticeship his master gave him a bag with a stick in it. If anyone were to mistreat him, all he had to do was say, "Now, stick, jump out of the bag," and the stick would beat his enemy until he said, "Now, into the bag again." The youngest son had heard about his brothers' misfortunes, so he went to the inn and told the innkeeper that he had a magical bag. In the night, the innkeeper crept into his room to steal it. At once the son shouted, "Now, stick, jump out of the bag," and it began to beat the thief until he cried out for mercy. "Only if you give back the magical donkey and table that you stole from my brothers," said the youngest son. Once the innkeeper had given him the table and donkey, the youngest son said, "Now, into the bag again," and off he went, leaving the innkeeper stiff and sore.

The tailor and his three sons lived very happily together, enjoying their riches and feasting every night. But the goat was so ashamed of her shaved head that she hid in a fox's den until the hair would grow back.

Spindle, Shuttle, Needle

Grimm, retold by Alice Mills

Once upon a time, there was an orphan girl who lived with her godmother, and they earned their living by spinning, weaving and sewing. The godmother grew very old and knew that she would soon die. She had no gold or silver to give the girl, only their cottage and the spindle for spinning thread, the shuttle for weaving cloth and the needle for sewing clothes. Now the orphan girl was all alone.

The prince of that country was looking for a bride, and he wanted her to be both the richest and the poorest of women. He looked all over the country, until at last he came to the orphan girl's village. The people told the prince where the wealthiest girl lived, and where the poor orphan girl lived.

The prince rode past the rich girl's house, and he could see at a glance that she was certainly very rich but not at all poor. Then he rode up to the poor orphan's house and looked in through the window, where he saw her hard at work. She was certainly poor, but was she rich as well? He rode away, wondering.

The orphan girl kept thinking about the handsome prince while she was spinning, and she soon began to sing some strange words that her godmother had taught her:

Spindle, spindle, run away,
Fetch my darling here today.

To her amazement, the spindle flew out of the door and away, leaving a trail of golden thread behind it all the way to the prince. So he began following the thread back to her.

As he was riding along, she sang again, this time to her shuttle:

Shuttle, shuttle, flying free,
Bring my darling home to me.

The shuttle jumped out of her hand and flew to the ground where it began to weave a magnificent carpet, embroidered with flowers and leaves, birds, deer and rabbits.

The orphan girl took out her needle to sew, and she began to sing yet again:

Needle, needle, sharp and keen,
Make my cottage neat and clean.

Up jumped the needle and flew to and fro. Not only was the cottage tidied and cleaned, but it started to look like a palace, with rich carpets and curtains, fine furniture and gleaming plates and dishes.

Just then the prince rode up, full of awe and wonder at the changes that had happened to the cottage. He said to the orphan girl, "You are truly both the poorest and the richest of girls, will you do me the great honor of becoming my bride?" So the little orphan girl was now a princess and lived happily ever after with her prince. She took the magical spindle, shuttle and needle with her to the palace where they became the kingdom's greatest treasures.

The Enchanted Stag

Grimm, retold by Alice Mills

There once was a man whose wife died. He married again, but his new wife was a wicked witch, cruel to the son and daughter of his first wife. One day the brother and sister ran away into the forest.

They took no food or drink with them, so they soon grew thirsty, but their stepmother had cast a spell over all the water in the forest. They came to a river where the brother wanted to drink, but his sister said, "Stop! Anyone who tastes this water will turn into a tiger." Then they came to a spring where the brother wanted to drink, but his sister said, "Stop! Anyone who tastes this water will turn into a wolf." Then they came to a stream, and the sister said, "Stop! Anyone who tastes this water will turn into a stag," but her brother was so thirsty that he drank from the stream. Instantly he turned into a stag. They cried, and then they found a deserted hut where they lived happily for a long time.

One day the king came to the forest to hunt deer. The brother heard the huntsmen, and longed to go out and see them. His sister said, "When you come back at night, knock at the door, saying, "Dear little sister, let me in." Off he went and the huntsmen chased him, but he escaped and came safely home.

The next day he heard the huntsmen and asked to go out again. Again he was hunted, but one of the king's servants followed him home and heard him say, "Dear little sister, let me in."

The third day, his sister let him go out to see the hunt again, and again he was hunted, but this time it was the king who knocked at the door and said, "Dear little

sister, let me in." He saw the beautiful girl and asked her to marry him. When she was married, she brought the stag to live in the palace with her.

Soon the king and queen had a baby. The wicked stepmother heard about her stepdaughter's happiness and came to the palace with her ugly daughter. They captured the queen and put the ugly daughter in her place, with a spell to stop the king noticing. But the queen escaped and that night she crept into the baby's room and nursed him in her arms. A servant noticed her there and told the king. The next night he stayed in the nursery and saw the true queen come in to nurse the baby.

This broke the spell and he took back his true queen. The wicked stepmother and her ugly daughter were banished from the kingdom, and the enchanted stag at once turned back into a handsome young man. He lived happily ever after, along with his sister the queen and her husband the king.

The Little Gray Man

Grimm, retold by Alice Mills

A man had two clever sons and the third son was a fool. The oldest son was a woodcutter, and every day his mother used to give him something good to eat and drink to take to the forest. One day he met a little gray man in the forest, who asked him for a little food and drink. "No, you insolent beggar," said the woodcutter, "if I gave you my food I would have none left for myself." So the old man went away and the woodcutter began cutting down trees. His axe slipped and he cut his arm, and this was all due to the little gray man.

The next day, the second son went into the forest to cut wood, and his mother gave him something good to eat and drink. He too met the little gray man and then refused to give him any food or drink. Then he cut his leg with the axe, and this was all due to the little gray man.

Then the foolish son said to his father, "Send me into the forest." His father did not want him to go, but finally he agreed. The boy's mother gave him only a nasty burnt cake and some water.

In the forest, he met the little gray man who asked for food and drink, and he looked in his basket to share the burnt cake and water. They had changed to delicious food and drink, and that was all due to the little gray man. As well, he gave the boy the gift of good luck, and ordered him to look among the roots of an old tree.

There he found a goose with feathers of pure gold. He was carrying it along the road when three sisters saw the golden goose and longed for its feathers. First the eldest of them touched its side. Her finger stuck to its wing and she could not get free.

Then her sister touched her and stuck fast and so did the third sister.

The boy walked off carrying the goose, and the three sisters had to follow along. They met peasants and soldiers, bakers and millers along the road, who all wanted to touch the goose and soon stuck fast, one after another. Then they all came to a city where the king's daughter didn't know how to laugh. The king said that the first man who could make her laugh could marry her. When she saw the line of people, all stuck to one another, she started to laugh.

The king did not want to marry her to a fool, so he said that the youngest son could only marry her if he found someone who could drink the royal cellar dry. Off went the boy into the forest, looking for the little gray man to help him, and there he found a miserable fellow complaining of thirst. "I have drunk the river dry," he said, "and I am still thirsty." So the boy took him to the king, and he drank the royal cellar dry.

But the king still did not want the boy to marry his daughter, so he said that first he must find someone who could eat a mountain of bread. Back went the boy into the forest, where he found a man complaining of hunger, even though he had just eaten a huge meal. The boy brought him to the king, and the man ate a mountain of bread and then asked for more.

The king then said that the boy must give him a ship that could travel by land as well as by water. Off went the boy into the forest, and there the little gray man gave him just such a ship. Then the king had no more excuses, and the boy married the princess and they lived happily ever after.

The Cottage in the Wood

Grimm, retold by Alice Mills

There was once a woodcutter with three daughters. One day he said to his oldest daughter, "Go and fetch me some food at noon. I will throw down a trail of seeds for you to follow."

So off she went into the forest with bread and soup for her father. But the sparrows had picked up all the seeds and she lost her way. On she walked into the night, and then she saw light streaming from a cottage window. She knocked at the door, and a very rough voice said, "Come in." Inside was an old man with a long white beard, together with a rooster, a hen and a cow. The girl asked to stay there for the night, and the animals nodded yes. Then the old man told her to cook supper. She cooked a meal for herself and the old man, but she forgot to feed the animals. Then the old man told her to make the beds. She

made the bed for herself, lay down on it and fell asleep. When the old man saw that his bed was not made, he opened a trapdoor underneath the girl's bed, so that it fell down swish swoosh into the cellar.

The next morning, the woodcutter told his second daughter to bring his lunch. Off she went into the forest, and she too got lost, because the birds had eaten the woodcutter's trail of seeds. She found the cottage in the dark, and met the old man and his three animals. Then she cooked a meal for herself and the old man but neglected the animals, and made a bed for herself but not for the old man. So swish, swoosh, she landed in the cellar just like her sister.

The next morning, the woodcutter told his third daughter to fetch his lunch. Off she went into the forest and she too got lost, because the birds had devoured all the seeds. She came to the cottage where the animals welcomed her, and then the old man told her to cook supper. First she fed the animals, and then she cooked supper for the old man and herself. When he told her to make the beds, first she gave the animals clean straw to sleep on, and then she made the old man's bed and last of all, she made her own bed.

In the morning she woke up to find that the cottage had changed into a palace and the old man into a handsome prince. He told her that a witch had enchanted him, and turned his servants into the three animals. The girl had broken the spell by her kindness to the animals. Then he asked for her hand in marriage. As for her sisters, they were set to work as servants until they learned to treat animals with kindness.

The Enchanted Tree

Grimm, retold by Alice Mills

A poor servant girl was once traveling through a wood with her master and mistress when they were attacked by robbers. The girl hid behind a tree, but her master and mistress were both killed.

When the robbers had gone, she could not find her way out of the forest, and grew so hungry and tired that she sat down under a tree. Then a white dove flew down with a little golden key in his beak. He said to her, "This key will unlock the door of the tree, where you will find all that you need." So she opened the door of the tree and found plenty to eat and drink.

Then she felt very weary. Down flew the dove with another key, and instructed her to unlock the door with it, and there she would find a fine bed to sleep on. And so she did.

In the morning the dove brought her a third key and told her that it would unlock the door of the tree containing fine clothes, fit for a princess.

She stayed in the wood for a long time, with the dove taking care of her. One day the dove asked her for help, saying, "I will take you to a cottage where an old woman is living. Say nothing to her. Instead, turn to the right and open the door and you will see a room full of precious rings. Bring me the plain gold ring, as fast as you can, and leave the rest."

So the girl followed the dove to the cottage. The old woman said, "Good day," but the girl did not reply. The old woman tried to stop her opening the door, but the girl went in and saw all the precious rings. She searched for the plain gold ring but could not find it. Then she noticed the old

woman slipping away with a birdcage in her hand. The girl ran after her and seized the cage, and when she looked inside, there was a bird with the plain ring in its beak.

She took the ring and went back in search of the dove, but she could not find him anywhere. Then she rested with her back against the tree, but suddenly its branches felt like arms holding her. It had become a handsome prince. He told her that the old woman was a wicked witch who had cast a spell on him, changing him into a tree. For two hours in the day, he could become a dove, but while she kept his ring, he could not become human again. Then he asked the girl to be his wife, and they went back to his kingdom where they lived happily ever after.

The Golden Castle of Stromberg

Grimm, retold by Alice Mills

There was once a little princess who was so naughty that one day her mother said, "I wish you were a raven and would fly away, and then I could have peace." No sooner had she uttered these fateful words than the princess changed into a raven and out through the window she flew to a dark wood. She remained there for a very long time, during which the mother and father heard nothing of her.

Years later, a man was traveling through this dark wood, when he heard a raven saying to him, "I am a princess by birth, and I need your help."

When he agreed to help the princess, she instructed him to go into a house in the forest where an old woman lived. She added that he must not eat or drink anything that the old woman offered him or he would fall into a deep sleep. The princess would arrive at two o'clock in the afternoon, and to break the spell he must be wide awake. She would try three times, and after that it would be much more difficult to rescue her.

So off he went to the house. When he got there the old woman offered him some water. He was thirsty and drank just a sip, but it made him so sleepy that he missed the princess's first visit. The next day the same thing happened, and on the third day he was so hungry that he forgot about the princess's instructions and ate all that the old woman offered him, and slept through the princess's final visit. This time, she left him a ring from her finger (on which her name was engraved), a meal of bread and cheese that he could never use up, and a letter saying that if he wished to rescue her, he must go to the golden castle of Stromberg.

The man asked everyone he met for directions to the castle. One day he came to the house of a giant, who threatened to eat him for dinner. "Why not have some of my food instead," said the man hastily. "There is more than enough here to satisfy even a giant's appetite." Then the giant showed the man a map; however, the golden castle of Stromberg was not there. The next day the giant's brother came home and this time the man fed both the giants, and the second giant lifted him up and carried him close to the golden castle.

It stood on a mountain of glass, and he could see the princess riding in her carriage just outside the castle, but the mountain was too steep and slippery for him to reach her. So he lived below in a little hut until he could find a way up the mountain.

One day he heard the sound of fighting. Three thieves were quarreling over how to share some magical items they had stolen: a stick that could open any door, a cloak that made its wearer invisible and a horse that could ride over any ground, even the glass mountain. When they saw the man, they asked him to decide. "Let me try them out first," replied the man, and he mounted the horse with the stick in hand and the cloak on his back. Then he rode off up the mountain, telling the thieves that he had decided to award everything to himself because he was the best thief of all.

He opened the castle door with his stick and found the princess. He gave her back the ring, and then he took off the cloak of invisibility. The princess kissed the man and declared that the spell was broken and they could be married and live happily forever.

The Good-tempered Tailor

Grimm, retold by Alice Mills

A good-tempered tailor once went traveling with a shoemaker, who was sour and grumpy. Whenever they went into a town, the tailor found it easy to get work, but the shoemaker was not so lucky. The tailor always shared what he had earned, so that they never went hungry.

One day they were traveling through a wood when they came to a fork in the path. They knew that one way took two days to reach the next town, and the other path took seven days, but they did not know which was which. The tailor had supplied himself with two days' worth of food, while the grumpy shoemaker was loaded down with seven days' worth. On the third day the tailor had nothing left to eat, but the shoemaker refused to share with him.

By the fourth day, the poor tailor could no longer bear his hunger and exhaustion, but the shoemaker would only feed him if the tailor gave him an eye in return. Sadly the tailor agreed. The next day he was hungry again, and the cruel shoemaker took his second eye in return for food. Then he abandoned the blind tailor in the forest.

The tailor then heard two birds talking, saying that the dew under their tree had the power to cure blindness, so in the morning he rubbed his face with dew and his eyes grew back as good as ever. Then he walked on, feeling hungry again.

He met a horse and caught it, so that he might ride to the next town, but the horse begged for his freedom. "A time may well come," the horse said, "when I can repay your kindness." So on the tailor walked. Then he caught a long-legged stork and made ready to kill and eat it, but the bird begged him for its freedom. "A time may come," the stork said, "when I can repay you." So on he walked, hungrily. Then he caught a duck, but the duck begged for her freedom and again promised to repay him one day. Finally, he found a hollow tree where the bees had stored honey, and he was just about to take the honeycomb when the queen bee warned him off. She too promised to repay his kindness one day.

When he came to the town, he soon got work, and very soon he became the royal tailor. The wicked shoemaker was also working at the palace, and he was jealous of the tailor's success and afraid that he might take revenge for the loss of his eyes. So he told the king that the tailor had been boasting that he could find the king's lost crown. The king ordered the tailor to produce the crown, and the poor tailor decided to run away. Back he went to the forest, where he met the duck. "That is easy," said the duck, diving into the stream, and she brought back the lost crown in her beak. So back the tailor went, and gave the crown to the king.

The next day, the shoemaker told the king that the tailor had boasted that he could build a model of the palace out of wax. The king demanded this model from the tailor, and back he ran to the forest. This time he met the queen bee, and she told him not to worry. By next morning the bees had built a wax model of the palace, and he carried it carefully to the king.

Then the shoemaker told the king that the tailor had boasted that he could build a fountain just outside the royal palace, in a single second. So the king ordered the tailor to achieve this, and back the tailor went to the forest. This time it was the horse who met him, and together they went to the palace where the horse stamped his foot on the ground. Up jetted a magnificent fountain, built in less than a second.

Then the shoemaker told the king that the tailor had claimed that he could provide a new royal baby within a day. The king promised his eldest daughter to the tailor if he could do this. Back the tailor ran to the forest, and this time it was the stork who came to his rescue. The stork told the tailor to wait at the castle on a certain day. On that day the tailor watched as the stork flew into the queen's bedroom with a new baby in his beak. And that is how the good-tempered tailor came to marry a princess, and lived with her happily ever after.

However, the wicked shoemaker was driven out of town into the forest, where both his eyes were scratched out by thorns, and he has never been heard of to this day.

Florinda and Yoringal

Grimm, retold by Alice Mills

Once upon a time there was a wicked fairy who lived in a castle deep in the wood. In the daytime she became an owl, at night a cat, but at twilight she was an old, old woman. If anyone came too close to her castle, she caught them with her magic. When a man came within her spell, suddenly he could no longer move his arms and legs, until she set him free. When a lovely young woman came too close, the wicked fairy changed her into a tiny bird, and kept her in a cage. There were seven thousand cages in the castle, full of these rare birds.

In a village nearby lived a handsome young man, Yoringal, who was in love with a beautiful young woman, Florinda. One evening they went for a walk together in the forest. As it grew dark, they lost their way and came much too close to the castle.

Florinda cried out sorrowfully as she suddenly changed into a nightingale. Yoringal could do nothing to help her, for he too was under a spell and could no longer move. He could only watch as the fairy put the bird in a cage and went back to her castle, leaving him alone in the dark wood.

Much later, the fairy returned and released him from the spell. He begged her to let Florinda go free again, but she only laughed at him. He went sadly away, trying to invent a way to free the trapped bird. One night he had a strange dream that he found a beautiful blood-red flower that destroyed all of the wicked fairy's power. In Yoringal's dream, when he took the flower to the castle and touched the cages all the birds became young women again.

When Yoringal woke up, he began to search everywhere for the blood-red flower. It took him nine long days of searching before he found it. He picked the flower and took it to the castle. At the touch of its petals, every door opened, and he found himself in a huge hall full of birdcages. He looked this way and that, trying to recognise his Florinda, but which of the birds was she? The wicked fairy could not use her magic against Yoringal, now that he had the flower in his hand. Instead, she tried to creep away with one of the bird cages in her hand. Yoringal ran after her, touching the bird with the petals of the flower, and suddenly the cage fell apart. There stood his beautiful Florinda.

Then Yoringal changed all the birds back into human form before he and Florinda went home, where they married and lived happily ever after.

White and Black

Grimm, retold by Alice Mills

One day a woman and her daughter and her stepdaughter were out walking, when they met a fairy disguised as a poor woman. She asked them to help her find her way. Both the mother and her daughter were rude to her, but the stepdaughter said, "I will show you the way."

Then the fairy cast a spell on the rude mother and daughter, making them blacker than night and so ugly that no one could bear to look at them. She offered the step-daughter three wishes. The young girl first wished to become a beautiful person. Then she asked for a purse that would never become empty. Finally, she asked to go to heaven when she died.

Now the stepdaughter had a brother, who was the king's coachman. He loved her dearly and asked for her portrait to hang in his room in the castle. The king of that country was looking for a wife. One day another servant saw the portrait in the coachman's room, and told the king how lovely she was. The king went to see for himself, and he fell in love and sent for her to be his bride, sending his royal carriage for her to ride in and splendid clothes for her to wear.

But the wicked woman (who was really a witch) and her daughter were jealous, and they demanded to go to the palace as well. First the wicked mother ordered her step-daughter and her own daughter to change clothes. Then she told them to change hats. And when the carriage stopped beside a river, the woman pushed her stepdaughter into the water and went on without her.

When the king looked into the carriage, he saw the ugliest woman. He was furious with the coachman and threw the poor man into prison. But the witch cast a spell on the king so he soon found the ugly daughter beautiful, and he decided to marry her.

A week before the wedding, a beautiful white duck came into the kitchen and asked to warm her feathers. She asked the kitchen maid for news of the wedding and then she flew away. The next night, the same thing happened. Then the kitchen maid told the king about the talking duck, and the next night he cut off the bird's head. Immediately she changed back into his beautiful bride. He released the coach-man from prison, and as for the wicked witch and her daughter, he said that unless they left the kingdom at once, he would put them to work for him as servants for the rest of their days. Off they fled, but the king and his bride lived happily ever after, and so did the royal coachman.

May Blossom

Grimm, retold by Alice Mills

There was once a queen who longed to have a daughter. One day, when she was in the bath, a frog popped out of the water and said, "Your wish will be granted, and you will have a baby daughter."

By the end of that year the king and queen had a lovely baby daughter. The king could scarcely contain his joy, and planned to celebrate with a huge feast. He invited all of his friends and relations, and also some wise women who would be able to give the baby magical gifts. There were thirteen of these wise women, but only twelve of them were invited. The king ordered that twelve golden plates be laid out for them.

At the end of the feast the wise women began to give the baby their gifts, starting with beauty, wisdom and wealth, but they were suddenly interrupted. In ran the thirteenth wise woman, furious at being left out, and she shouted, "When this baby is fifteen, she will prick her finger with a spindle and drop dead!" And without another word she stormed out of the hall.

There was only one wise woman who had not yet given her gift to the princess, and she could not take away all the power of this curse, but she said, "The child will not die. She will fall into a deep sleep for a hundred years."

The baby grew as beautiful as may blossom, so that is what everyone called her. The king and queen ordered all spindles in the kingdom to be burned. They could do nothing more to protect their daughter.

As she grew up, May Blossom loved exploring the castle. One day she found an old tower with a narrow, winding staircase leading to a little wooden door. In the lock was a rusty old key, and as she turned it the door flew open. Inside sat an old woman spinning flax with a spindle in her hand.

"What is that strange thing you hold in your hand?" asked the princess, who had never before seen anyone spinning. "Come here and see," said the old woman, and the princess touched the spindle. Immediately the wicked woman's prophecy was fulfilled and the princess fell into a very deep sleep, and so did the king and queen and everyone else in the castle. Even the horses in the stable, the dogs in the yard and the pigeons in the roof fell into a deep slumber. And the fire in the hearth suddenly became still.

Over the many years, a tall hedge of thorns grew up around the sleeping castle. Now and then a prince would try to get through, but without success.

Finally, one hundred years later, a handsome prince came to the thorn hedge. To his surprise the hedge was now covered with beautiful large flowers, which opened up a path for the prince to the castle. As he walked through the path the hedge closed again behind him.

Everything was still and silent inside the court of the castle, all the birds and animals asleep, as well as all the people. The prince wandered from room to room until he found the tower where the beautiful May Blossom lay asleep. As soon as set eyes on her, the prince fell in love with her and bent down to kiss her. At once the wicked spell was broken and the lovely young princess woke up. Then the whole castle sprang to life again, and very soon the prince and princess were married with great splendor, and lived happily ever after.

The Good Bargain

Grimm, retold by Alice Mills

A peasant sold his cow at the market for seven dollars. On his way home, some frogs were croaking in a pond. It sounded to him like "eight, eight". You are wrong," he shouted, "it was seven dollars," but they kept on croaking "eight, eight". The man angrily threw his money into the pond so they could count it for themselves. He thought the frogs would throw the money back but they just kept up their croaking.

Then he took some meat to sell to the butcher. The butcher was not in his shop and a pack of dogs started sniffing at the meat. The peasant said to the butcher's dog, "If I leave this meat here, make sure that your friends do not touch it." The dog yapped "yap!" and the peasant thought he was saying "yes". So he put the meat on the counter and left. When he returned, the butcher refused to pay him, because the dogs had eaten the meat. Instead, he gave the peasant a beating.

So the peasant asked the king for help. He explained about the frogs taking his money and the dogs taking his meat and the butcher beating him, and the king's daughter began to laugh.

Then the king told the peasant that the princess had never laughed until now, and that he had promised to marry her to the first man who could make her laugh.

But the peasant said that he already had a wife at home, and one wife was more than enough. So the king offered him a reward instead, of five hundred dollars. "Come back tomorrow," he said, "and collect your money."

The peasant walked happily away. The palace sentinel asked what had happened and when he heard about the reward, he asked for two hundred dollars of it, and the peasant agreed. A moneylender overheard them, and he said that he would lend the peasant the rest of the money in advance, for a fee. So the moneylender gave him three hundred dollars, but took back almost all of it in fees.

Next day, the king had the money ready, but the peasant said to him, "None of that is mine. Two hundred dollars go to the sentinel and the rest to the moneylender."

The king was angry with the sentinel and the moneylender and told the peasant he had acted foolishly. "Try again," he said. "Fill your pockets with money from my treasury." The peasant did as he was told, but worried that he had taken too much. If only the king had said how much to take!

When the moneylender heard this he informed the king that the peasant was speaking ill of him. So the king called back the peasant to punish him, and the moneylender started to worry that the king might punish them both, so he offered to lend the peasant a coat. Then the king would see how generous he was, and perhaps reward him instead.

The peasant put on the coat and went to see the king who said, "The moneylender says that you speak ill of me." The peasant replied, "He is a liar! He will probably tell you that this coat belongs to him." "It does!" shouted the moneylender, but the king did not believe him. He sent them both away, and the peasant left wearing the moneylender's good coat, with his pockets full of money. "This time, at least," he said to himself, "I have made a good bargain."

Robinson Crusoe

Defoe, retold by Alice Mills

Robinson Crusoe was a young Englishman who went to sea, hoping to make his fortune. His first few voyages made him a rich man, but then he went back to sea, setting sail for the coast of Africa. In the middle of a most terrible storm, the ship was carried far away from her route and then, just after the watchman had called out, "Land!" she struck a sandbank. The sailors lowered a boat and desperately tried to row to safety, but a huge wave carried Robinson Crusoe overboard. The poor young man was washed up on an unknown shore, and found himself all alone.

The ship was stuck fast, but still above water. Crusoe built a little raft, and on it he carried to shore all the food in the ship. Next he rescued the ship's cats and dogs and some bags of seeds. He salvaged all the tools he could find, and made sure he took some weapons. Then he loaded the raft with clothes, hammock, rope and anything else he could carry, taking it to shore and then rowing back again for more as fast as he could, for he knew that the ship would soon become submerged.

Crusoe built himself a little house from wood and sailcloth, and there he lived snugly. He soon went exploring the land where he had been shipwrecked, and discovered that it was an island, with no other human inhabitants. There were plenty of wild goats, and Crusoe decided to catch and tame a few, so that he could have their company and their milk, and even try to make cheeses. Eventually, he had a whole flock of goats, and when his clothes wore out, he made new ones out of goatskin. He had not had the opportunity to bring any needles and thread from the ship, and so his stitches were big and clumsy, but at least these new clothes did not fall apart. Crusoe looked very odd in his hairy goatskin clothes and hat, and his goatskin umbrella looked odder still.

It took Crusoe another five years to succeed in building a little canoe that he could carry down to the shore. This boat was far too small to sail across the sea to reach the mainland, but now, at least, he would be able to sail all the way round the island.

One day, at about noon, Crusoe was going to his boat when he noticed the print of a man's naked foot on the shore. He was amazed and wonder-struck, and went this way and that, looking, listening, but no-one was there. He went home fearfully imagining human shapes in every bush and tree, terrified of shadows.

Crusoe frightened himself still more by imagining that a boatload of Africans might be searching the island for him, ready to loot his possessions and leave him to starve. But for days and weeks, there was no sign of any visitors, friendly or hostile. Then he began to think more sensibly. For fifteen years he had lived alone on the island. If people had come from the mainland, it could only have been for a short while. Perhaps these visitors had been driven off course in a storm and were eager to get home again. They might not pose the slightest threat to his flock of goats or his precious field of wheat.

When he was first shipwrecked, he was so busy collecting items from the ship that he did not keep count of the days, but after ten days or so he began to keep a record. He set up a square post on the shore where he had landed, and on it he carved a notch for each day, and a longer notch to mark each week, and then each month.

As the months and years went by, he became skilled in making cheese and growing crops, hunting and fishing. He taught himself how to make pots out of clay and bake them in the sun, and how to make furniture. His most ambitious project was to build himself a boat. The first boat he built was so big and heavy that he could not pull it down to the water, and the second boat was built a long way from shore, with a hill in between, and so that boat was never launched. By now Crusoe had lived on the island for four years.

Crusoe thought that it would be a good idea to choose a lookout spot, and so he found a hill with a splendid view over the ocean. Occasionally, over the years, he saw boats in the distance, and once he witnessed Africans coming to shore, but he always felt too afraid to go near them. One night he dreamed of visiting Africans who started to fight one another until he rescued one of them. In the morning, his dream started to come true. There on the shore were at least thirty Africans, and two of them seemed to be prisoners. Suddenly one of the prisoners ran away along the beach.

The captive started to run straight towards Crusoe's hill, and only three men gave chase. When they all came to a fast-flowing stream, the captive swam across, but only two of his pursuers followed him. Crusoe gathered up his courage and stepped out of his hiding place. The two men took one look at the hairy monster confronting them and ran away. Soon all the boats were in the water, sailing as fast as they could for the mainland.

Crusoe beckoned to the prisoner to come closer. The man walked cautiously up to him, smiling in gratitude and speaking in a language that Crusoe did not understand. But the words were very sweet to his ear, for they were the first human speech he had heard for twenty-five years.

Crusoe called the man Friday, as this was the day on which he had been rescued. Friday became a loyal servant and friend to Robinson Crusoe. He learned how to speak English, make pots and bake wheat loaves, and Crusoe sewed him a selection of hairy goatskin clothes.

One day Friday came running towards Crusoe, shouting, "A ship! A ship!" Crusoe raced up the hill until he could see the ship plainly. It was an English sailing ship lying at anchor close to shore. He noticed that some sailors went off in search of food and fresh water, and some were left behind. Clearly there had been a mutiny. Once

the sailors on shore had all left, Crusoe and Friday ran down to free the prisoners. Crusoe saw how they shrank away from the sight of these two hairy creatures, and whispered, "Gentlemen, don't be surprised at me: you may indeed have a friend near, when you did not expect it." He was over-joyed when they replied in English. At last, Crusoe had a chance of returning home.

Friday and Crusoe quickly rescued the prisoners then rowed back to the ship, leaving the mutineers marooned but leaving Crusoe's diary for them to read, with all the information they'd need to survive there. The ship then set sail for England. Robinson Crusoe had lived on the island for twenty-eight years, two months and nineteen days.

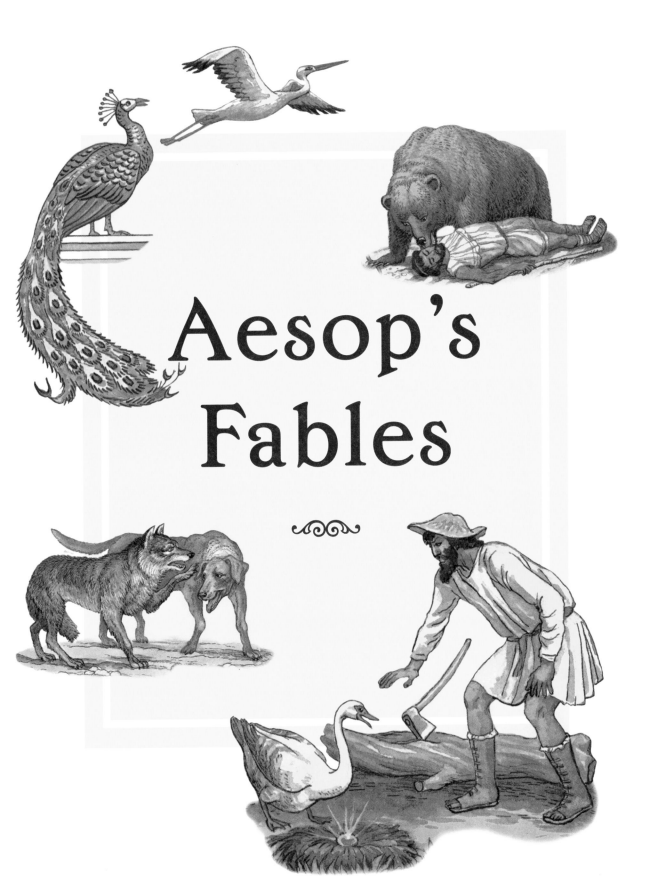

Aesop's Fables

One winter's day a Woodcutter found a Snake under a hedge, almost dead from cold. He wrapped the Snake in his jacket and brought it home, putting it by the fire to warm it up. The Snake soon became lively again, and reared up to strike at the Woodcutter's wife and children, filling the cottage with its hissing. The Woodcutter seized his axe and cut off the Snake's head, saying, "Is this the reward you offer the man who saved your life? Die as you deserve!"

The wicked give no thanks.

The Woodcutter and the Snake

The Horse and the Donkey

A Warhorse came thundering down the road. He overtook a Donkey who was struggling to pull a heavy cart. "Move over and let me pass," demanded the Horse, "or I promise I shall trample you into the dust." The poor Donkey moved out of the way silently. Later, the Horse was wounded in battle. His master sold him to a carter, and now the Horse had to pull a heavy cart.

One day the Donkey met him on the road and said, "Is that you, my friend? How true it is that

Pride comes before a fall."

A feeble Old Man went into the forest to pick up sticks for his fire. Afterwards he was too weary to walk home. He began to ask Death to take him and give him rest. Death suddenly appeared in front of the Old Man. The Old Man was terrified, and he certainly did not want to die. "I dropped my bundle of sticks," he said, "and when I knelt down to pick them up I was too tired to stand up again. Please help me stand up, your majesty, that is all I want!"

Be careful what you wish for.

The Old Man and Death

The Bear and the Bees

A Bear found a hollow tree, in which a swarm of Bees had made their home. Inside the hollow was a mass of honey. The Bear started to climb the tree to steal the honey, but a Bee came flying home and saw what he was doing. She decided to sting him, and give her life in defence of her sisters. The Bear was furious with the pain of the sting, and attacked the tree with his claws, trying to tear open the little hole and destroy all the Bees. The whole swarm came buzzing out at him, and the Bear fell and was forced to run away in search of a pond, where he could cover himself in water and keep himself safe from their stings.

Anger is its own worst enemy.

A small thin Mouse gnawed a little hole in a basket of corn. He climbed in and ate until his stomach bulged. When he tried to climb out again, his stomach was too fat to fit through the hole. A Weasel watched him struggling and laughed at him, saying, "If you want to escape, there is only one way. You must become as poor and thin as you were before you climbed into the basket, and then you will fit your stomach through the hole again."

Take only what you need.

The Mouse and the Weasel

The Serpent and the Eagle

An Eagle caught a Serpent in her claws and tried to fly away with him. The Serpent wound his coils around her so that she could not fly. They were twined together so closely that neither could win the fight. A Peasant came over and pulled the Serpent away so that the Eagle could use her beak. She soon killed the Serpent, but as he lay dying he spat poison into the Peasant's cup. The Eagle knocked the cup out of his hand so that the poison spilled out without harming anything.

In times of trouble you know your true friends.

A Farmer was sowing his field with flax. The Birds were busy picking up seeds to eat. The Swallow said to the other Birds, "Make sure that you eat every seed, for flax seeds produce thread that is woven into nets to catch birds." The Birds paid him no attention. The flax grew and was harvested, and then the threads were made into nets that caught the foolish Birds. "If only you had listened to me," said the Swallow as he flew away.

Destroy the seeds of evil before it is too late.

The Swallow and the Other Birds

The Lioness and the Vixen

A Lioness and a Vixen were talking about their children. "We Foxes are the happiest of animals," boasted the Vixen, "for when we have children they are always twins or triplets or even more. I feel sorry for other animals who have only one child. How many children do you have?" she asked the Lioness, knowing that there was only one Lion cub.

The Lioness said angrily, "I have only one child and you have many. But all your children will grow up to be nothing but Foxes. My child will grow up to be king of the animals."

Quality is better than quantity.

One morning, while the Bees were out gathering honey, a thief came to the hive and smashed it so that he could steal the honey. The Bee-keeper found his hive in ruins and all the honey stolen. The Bees flew home, laden with honey, and at once they began to sting the Bee-keeper. "What are you doing now?" he shouted. "You let the thief escape, and now you are stinging the man who has always cared for you. How ungrateful you all are!"

Make sure you punish the right person.

The Bee-keeper

The Frog and the Fighting Bulls

A Frog peeped out of the lake and noticed two Bulls fighting in the meadow a long way away. He called to his friends, "That terrible fight will bring disaster to us!"

The other Frogs said, "The Bulls are fighting to find out who will lead the herd. Their quarrel has nothing to do with us."

"That is true," said the first Frog, "but the Bull who loses the fight will have to leave the meadow, and he may come here, and then he might trample some of us to death!"

When great people quarrel, little people get hurt.

The Weasels and the Mice were at war. The Weasels always won, for they were bigger and stronger. The Mice thought that they were losing the war because their army had no commanders. So they chose the biggest Mice as commanders, and gave them tall helmets with plumes made out of grass stalks, so that they could be recognised in battle. The next time they fought, the Mice lost again. They all ran to their holes and escaped, except for the commanders, whose helmets could not fit into the holes.

Greatness has its price.

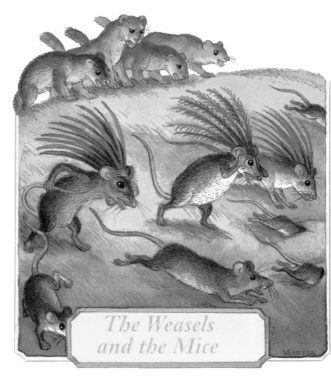

The Weasels
and the Mice

The Hawk
and the
Nightingale

A Hawk was looking for prey when he heard a Nightingale singing. He dived down and caught her in his talons. "I am such a small bird," said the Nightingale. "Let me go, and catch a bigger bird who will make you a better meal."

"I have been searching for something to eat all day," replied the Hawk. "Now you want me to let you go in the hope of finding something better. If I did what you ask, which one of us would be the fool?"

A bird in the hand is worth two in the bush.

A Lion became old and ill. Everyone visited, except the Fox. The Wolf said to the Lion, "The wicked Fox does not care if you live or die."

Just then the Fox arrived. He quickly told the Lion, "I have been busy finding a cure for you. You must kill a Wolf and wrap yourself in his skin to keep warm." The Lion did so, and the Fox said to himself, "That is a bad end to a bad animal. It was the Wolf's fault for spreading lies about me."

Ill will breeds ill will.

The Lion, the Wolf and the Fox

The Horse and the Stag

The Horse and the Stag ate grass together until they quarreled. The Stag drove the Horse away from the grass with his sharp horns. Then the Horse asked the Man to help him drive away the Stag. The Man promised to help, if he could saddle the Horse, put a bridle in his mouth and ride him. They easily drove away the Stag, and then the Horse asked the Man to set him free. "No," replied the Man. "Now that I know just what a good servant you are, I shall never set you free."

Do not give away your freedom.

An Ant fell into a stream one day. A Dove saw the Ant drowning and pulled a leafy twig from a tree, dropping it into the water so that the Ant could climb onto a leaf. Then the twig floated safely ashore. Later, a man laid nets beside the stream to catch birds. The Dove flew down, looking for seeds, and was in danger of being caught. The Ant ran up the man's shoe and bit his ankle, so that he cried out in pain. The Dove was warned and flew safely away.

One good turn deserves another.

The Dove and the Ant

The Travelers and the Bear

Two Travelers promised to help each other if they met any danger. Suddenly a Bear rushed at them. One man was strong and quick, and he climbed a tree. The other was slow and clumsy. He fell down and lay there holding his breath. The Bear sniffed at him, thought he was dead, and went off without hurting him. "What did the Bear say to you?" asked the other man from up in his tree.

The man on the ground answered, "He told me to put no trust in cowards like you."

A friend in need is a friend indeed.

A Carter was driving a heavily laden cart along a muddy lane. The wheels sank into the mud until the cart stuck fast. The Carter did nothing but weep and wail for help to Hercules the strong. The hero appeared, looking down at him from a cloud. "Why are you making such a noise?" he asked. "Do not lie there in the dirt like a lazy fool. Stand up and help your horses. Put your shoulder to the wheel. That is the only help that I will give you."

Heaven helps those who help themselves.

Hercules and the Carter

The Young Man and the Swallow

A foolish Young Man was walking by a stream one winter's day. The sun shone and a Swallow flew over the water, believing that it was summer. The Young Man also believed that summer had come. He sold his heavy winter clothes and spent the money on drink and gambling. Then he went back to the river, where the Swallow lay dead on the ice. "If only I had not believed your news," he said to the Swallow, "I would not have sold my clothes and lost all my money."

One swallow does not make a summer.

A Crow was half dead with thirst when he found a pitcher. The Crow put his beak in, but there was only a little water at the bottom. He could not reach far enough to drink. He tried and tried, and was about to give up when he noticed that the ground was covered with pebbles. He dropped a pebble into the pitcher, then another and another, and another, until at last the water was up near the mouth of the pitcher. Now he could put his beak in and drink his fill.

Little by little does the trick.

The Crow and the Pitcher

The Lion, Jupiter and the Elephant

The Lion fears only one thing, the sound of a rooster crowing. One day he asked Jupiter to cure him of that, but the god refused. "What is the matter?" asked the Elephant, seeing the Lion in tears. The Lion explained, but the Elephant did not listen. He kept glancing away, until the Lion asked what was troubling him. The Elephant replied, "I am terrified that a tiny gnat will fly into my ear, and kill me." At once the Lion felt happier, for a rooster is a much bigger threat than a gnat.

Troubles are rarely as bad as they seem.

A Stag ran into the farmyard to escape from some Dogs, and buried himself in a heap of straw in the stable. Only his antlers stuck out. In came a servant to feed the Horses, and then a groom to brush their coats, but they paid no attention to the straw in the corner. The Stag felt safe now, but in came the owner of both Horses and stable, and he noticed the antlers at once. He called his men to take hold of the poor Stag and kill him.

No-one looks after your business as well as you.

The Stag in the Stable

The Ant and the Grasshopper

One summer's day a Grasshopper was singing and dancing, while an Ant was dragging an ear of wheat along to his nest. It was so heavy that he could hardly move it. "Why not forget your work and have fun with me instead?" said the Grasshopper.

"I am storing food for the winter," replied the Ant, "and you should do so too."

"But I've enough food for today," said the Grasshopper, and off he went.

In the winter the Ants had plenty of food in their nest, but the Grasshopper had no food and was dying of hunger.

Take thought for tomorrow.

The Peacock met the Crane one day. The Peacock spread his tail and moved his body so that all his long feathers could be seen at their best. "What an ordinary bird you are," he said to the Crane, "with no splendid tail feathers to boast of."

The Crane replied, "Peacocks would be fine birds indeed, if fine feathers were all that mattered. But it is far better to fly above the clouds like a Crane than to be stuck on the ground like a poor Peacock."

Fine feathers do not make fine birds.

A Frog climbed out of the swamp and began croaking a message to all the other animals. "If you are ill, if you have aches and pains and broken bones, come to me," he called out. "I know how to heal you all, for I am a doctor."

The animals all believed him, except for the Fox. "Look at this miserable Frog," said the Fox to the other animals. "His skin is covered with blotches and his voice is nothing but a croak. If he is such a good doctor, why has he not healed himself?"

Doctor, heal yourself.

The Lion was the best of kings, most gentle and kind. He was never cruel, and he never let anger overpower him. He was just and fair, taking care of all the animals alike. He called all his subjects together and told them that he had made a new law. They must all now live in peace together, the Tiger and the Deer, the Fox and the Hunting Dog, the Wolf and the Lamb. The little animals, weak and timid, said to their king, "This is the day we have longed for."

Dreams can come true.

A Donkey and a Fox went hunting together. They were terrified when they saw a Lion. The cunning Fox ran towards the Lion and whispered, "I can trap the Donkey, to save you the trouble of chasing him, if you will let me go free." The Lion agreed. The Fox led the Donkey to a hidden pit. The Donkey fell in, and the Lion came along to thank the Fox. Suddenly the Lion attacked the Fox and killed him, knowing that the Donkey was trapped and could not run away.

Betray your friend and you may betray yourself.

A Queen Bee flew to Jupiter's palace to give him a present of honey. The god was so pleased that he promised to give anything that she asked, as a reward. She asked him to give every Bee a sting that would kill, so that they could defend their honey. Jupiter was not pleased to hear this, but he had to keep his promise. "Here are your stings," he said. "They will help you defend your hives, but whenever a Bee uses her sting, it is the Bee who will die."

Evil is its own punishment.

The Bee and Jupiter

The Stag and His Reflection

A Stag saw himself reflected in the water. "What magnificent antlers I have," he said, "but my legs are thin and weak." Just then he heard the sound of the hunt, and began to run from the Dogs. In the open, he was faster than any Dog. In the wood, his antlers became tangled in branches, and the Dogs pulled him down. "My magnificent antlers caused me death," the Stag said with his last breath, "yet my thin weak legs were the only thing that could have saved me."

What is worth the most is often valued the least.

101

The Flies found their way into a kitchen where a jar of honey had been left open. Down flew all the Flies, greedy for the sweet honey, but they did not notice how sticky it was. When they tried to fly away, their feet stuck fast to the jar. No matter how hard they tried, their wings could not lift them into the air. "How foolish we are," the Flies buzzed to one another. "We have lost our freedom for nothing more than a little drop of honey."

Pleasures are sometimes bought too dearly.

The Flies and the Honey

The Wolf and the Crane

A Wolf was eating his prey, when a bone stuck in his throat. He promised a handsome reward to any creature who would help him. The Crane wanted the reward. He told the Wolf to open his mouth wide, stuck his long beak down and pulled the bone free. "Now give me my reward," said the Crane.

The Wolf replied, "How dare you ask for a second reward; I had your head in my mouth and did not bite it off—and still you are not contented."

Gratitude does not go well with greed.

A Gardener's Dog once fell into a hole. The Gardener ran over to help him, and was just about to lift him out when the Dog bit his hand. The Gardener walked away angrily, leaving the Dog stuck in the hole. "You are a wicked Dog," he said, "to bite the hand that is busy saving your life, the hand of your master who has fed and cared for you! Die as you deserve, for such a mischievous and bad-natured creature does not deserve to live."

Do not bite the hand that feeds you.

The Gardener and His Dog

Jupiter and the Monkey

Jupiter, the king of the gods, held a competition to judge which animal had the most beautiful baby. Among the animals was a Monkey with a baby in her arms. He had very little hair, his nose had not yet grown properly, and he looked very unattractive. The gods began to laugh at the baby Monkey, and the other fathers and mothers shrank away. The Monkey mother held her baby close to her, and said, "I do not care what you think. In my eyes, my baby is the most beautiful of all."

Nothing is stronger than a mother's love.

The Hares were so badly treated by the other animals that they ran away whenever any other animal came near. One day they ran from a herd of wild horses. Off they ran to a lake, and they felt so miserable that they thought drowning themselves would be the best idea. As they came close to the water, they scared a host of Frogs that hopped away as fast as they could and jumped into the water. "Things are not nearly as bad as we thought," said one of the Hares,

"There is always someone worse off than yourself."

The Frogs and the Hares

The Lion and the Three Bulls

Three Bulls were friends. They always stayed close to each other and ate grass together. A Lion wanted to kill and eat them. He could have killed a single Bull easily, but not all three together. The Lion began to whisper to each of them in turn, telling lies about the others. His plan worked well. The Bulls became jealous of each other and began to graze in different parts of the field. Now the Lion found it easy to seize the Bulls one by one and devour them.

When friends quarrel, enemies get their chance.

A Farmer discovered a pot of gold half buried in his field. He ran to the temple of the Earth Goddess to thank her. The Goddess Fortune was furious, and appeared to him in the field. "Foolish man," she said, "why do you thank the Earth Goddess for a treasure that I gave you? You never considered that Fortune was with you when you found the pot of gold, but if you ever lose your wealth, you will put all the blame on your bad fortune."

Give thanks where thanks are owed.

The Farmer and Fortune

The Old Hunting Dog

A Hunting Dog grew old and weak and lost his teeth. One day Hunters and Hunting Dogs were chasing a Stag who ran until he escaped. The Stag stopped to rest, and all the young Dogs ran past without seeing him. Then the old Hunting Dog came slowly along. He took hold of the Stag's leg, but he had no teeth to bite with, and the Stag easily escaped again. The Hunting Dog said to his master, "Do not punish me. I am old and feeble, but still just as faithful as when I was young and strong."

Punish faults, not failings.

A Lion fell in love with a Peasant's Daughter and asked to marry her. The Peasant wanted to say no, but he was afraid of the Lion. "Your majesty," he said, "my Daughter fears that your claws and teeth might hurt her when you hug and kiss her. Let me trim your claws and pull out your teeth before the wedding." The Lion agreed, but as soon as his teeth and claws were gone, the Peasant beat him out of the house. Now the Lion saw that love had turned him into a fool.

Love tames even the wildest.

The Lion in Love

The Trees and the Peasant

A Peasant was looking around in a wood. The Trees asked him what he was looking for. "A straight piece of wood," said the Peasant, "to mend my axe handle." All the Trees wanted to help. The Ash Tree, who grew the straightest branches, dropped one at his feet. The Peasant nailed the Ash branch to his axe blade and began to cut down all the Trees.

The Oak Tree, waiting for the axe to strike, whispered to the Elm, "Brother, we must put up with this treatment, for we deserve it."

Do not help your enemy to hurt you.

An Owl was trying to sleep after her night's hunting. In the grass below, a Grasshopper kept her awake, insulting her, telling her that she was a strange and nasty bird. The Owl told the Grasshopper to be quiet, but he kept on chirping. Then she said, "I am starting to enjoy talking to you, because your voice is so beautiful. Come a little closer, please, and I will give you some water. You must be thirsty by now." The Grasshopper was very thirsty, and he jumped towards the tree. At once the Owl swooped down and ate him.

Do not push your luck.

The Owl and the Grasshopper

The Dog and the Wolf

A House-Dog was talking to a hungry Wolf. "If you want food," said the Dog, "why not share my work and my food. My master feeds me well every day."

The Wolf agreed, but as they walked along, he noticed that the hair on the Dog's neck was worn away. "What has happened?" he asked.

"That is only the place where my collar and chain go every night," said the Dog.

"Thank you for the offer of food," replied the hungry Wolf, "but I want nothing to do with any collars or chains."

Better starving and free than a fat slave.

Two Frogs began to complain to each other about the summer's heat. All of the lakes and ponds were almost dry. The Frogs agreed to travel together in search of water. They found a deep well, and both Frogs longed to jump in and enjoy the cool water far below. One of the Frogs sat on the brink, ready to jump. His friend hesitated and asked, "If the water in the well dries up like all the lakes and ponds that were once so full of water, how could we climb out?"

Think twice before you act.

The Frogs and the Well

The Hawk and the Farmer

A Hawk was chasing a Pigeon across a wheat field. He did not notice the net stretched out to catch crows. Straight into the net flew the Hawk, and the Farmer ran over to kill him. "Do not kill me," screeched the Hawk. "I am not a nasty crow! I do no harm to your crops! All I wanted to do was to catch and kill that plump Pigeon for my dinner."

"And what harm did the Pigeon do to you?" replied the Farmer, as he wrung the Hawk's neck.

Put yourself in the other person's shoes.

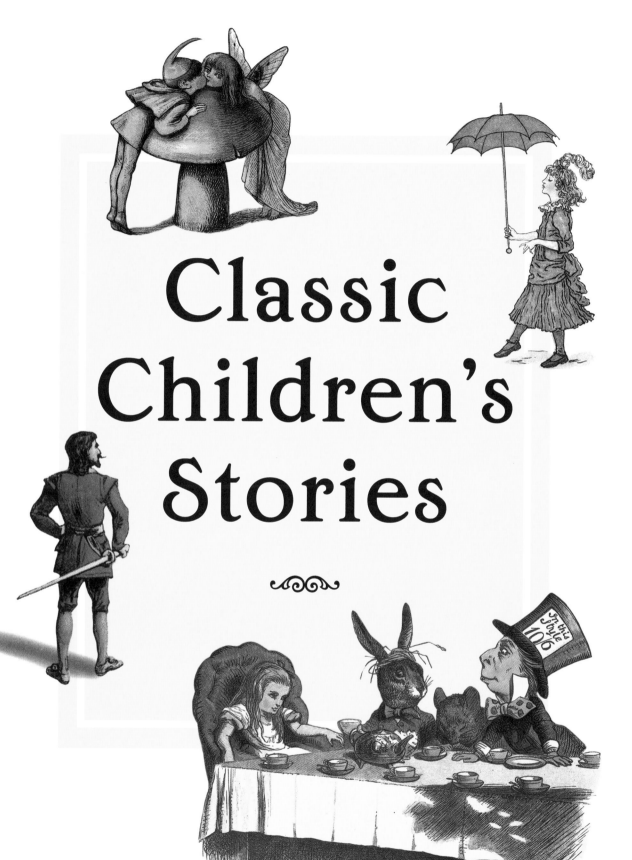

Classic Children's Stories

❦❦❦

Alice's Adventures in Wonderland

Lewis Carroll

1. THE WHITE RABBIT

Once upon a time, there was a little girl called Alice who had a most curious dream. Would you like to hear what it was that she dreamed about?

Well, this was the very *first* thing that happened. A White Rabbit came running by, in a great hurry; and, just as it passed Alice, it stopped and took its watch out of its pocket.

Wasn't *that* a funny thing? Did *you* ever see a Rabbit that had a watch, and a pocket to put it in? Of course, when a Rabbit has a watch it *must* have a pocket to put it in: it would never do to carry it about in its mouth— and it wants its hands sometimes, to run about with.

Hasn't it got pretty pink eyes (I think *all* White Rabbits have pink eyes); and pink ears; and a nice brown coat; and you can just see its red pocket-handkerchief peeping out of its coat-pocket; and, what with its blue neck-tie and its yellow waistcoat, it really is *very* nicely dressed.

"Oh dear, oh dear!" said the Rabbit. "I shall be too late!" *What* would it be too late *for,* I wonder? Well, you see, it had to go and visit the Duchess (you will see a picture of the Duchess soon, sitting in her kitchen); and the Duchess was a very cross old lady; and the Rabbit *knew* she would be very angry indeed if he kept her waiting. So the poor little thing was as frightened as frightened could be (Don't you see how he's trembling? Just shake the book a little from side to side and you'll soon see him tremble), because he thought the Duchess would have his head cut off, as punishment. That was what the Queen of Hearts used to do when *she* was angry with people (you'll see a picture of *her* soon); at least she used to *order* their heads to be cut off, and she always *thought* that it was done, though they never *really* did it.

And so, when the White Rabbit ran away, Alice wanted to see what would happen to it; so she ran after it: and she ran, and she ran, till she tumbled right down the rabbit-hole.

And then she had a very long fall indeed. Down, and down, and down, till she began to wonder if she was going right *through* the world, so as to come out on the other side!

It was just like a very deep well; only there was no water in it. If anybody *really* had such a fall as that it would kill them, most likely; but you know it doesn't hurt a bit to fall in a *dream,* because all the time you *think* you're falling, you really *are* lying somewhere, safe and sound, and fast asleep of course!

However, this terrible fall came to an end at last, and down came Alice on a heap of sticks and dry leaves. But she wasn't a bit hurt, and up she jumped, and ran after the Rabbit again.

And so that was the beginning of Alice's most curious dream. And, next time you see a White Rabbit, try and fancy that *you're* going to have a curious dream, just like dear little Alice.

2. HOW ALICE GREW TALL

And so, after Alice had tumbled down the rabbit-hole, and had run a long, long way underground, all of a sudden she found herself in a great hall, with doors all round it.

But all the doors were locked: so, you see, poor Alice couldn't get out of the hall; and that made her very sad.

After a little while, however, she came to a little table, all made of glass, with three legs (There are *two* of the legs in the picture, and just the *beginning* of the other leg, do you see?), and on the table was a little key; and she went round the hall and tried to see if she could unlock any of the doors with it.

Poor Alice! The key wouldn't unlock *any* of the doors. But at last she came to a tiny little door; and oh, how glad she was, when she found that the key would fit it!

So she unlocked the tiny little door, and she stooped down and looked through it, and what do you think she saw? Oh, such a beautiful garden! And she did so *long* to go into it! But the door was *far* too small. She couldn't squeeze herself through, any more than *you* could squeeze yourself into a mouse-hole!

So poor little Alice locked up the door, and took the key back to the table again: and *this* time she found quite a new thing on it (now look at the picture again), and what do you think it was? It was a little bottle, with a label tied to it, with the words "DRINK ME" on the label.

So she tasted it, and it was *very* nice; so she set to work, and drank it up. And then *such* a curious thing happened to her! You'll never guess what it was, so I shall have to tell you. She got smaller, and smaller, till at last she was just the size of a little doll!

Then she said to herself "*Now* I'm the right size to get through the little door!" And away she ran. But, when she got there, the door was locked, and the key was on the top of the table, and she couldn't reach it! *Wasn't* it a pity she had locked up the door again?

Well, the next thing she found was a little cake; and it had the words "EAT ME" marked on it. So of course she set to work and ate it up. And *then* what do you think happened to her? No, you'll never guess! I shall have to tell you again.

She grew, and she grew, and she grew. Taller than she was before! Taller than *any* child! Taller than any grown-up person! Taller, and taller, and taller! Just look at the picture, and you'll *see* how tall she got!

Which would *you* have liked the best, do you think, to be a little tiny Alice, no larger than a kitten, or a great tall Alice, with your head constantly knocking against the ceiling?

3. THE POOL OF TEARS

Perhaps you think Alice must have been very much pleased, when she had eaten the little cake, to find herself growing so tremendously tall? Because of course it would be easy enough, *now*, to reach the little key off the glass table, and to open the little tiny door.

Well, of course she could do *that;* but what good was it to get the door open, when she couldn't get *through?* She was worse off than ever, poor thing! She could just manage, by putting her head down, close to the ground, to *look* through with one eye! But that was *all* she could do. No wonder the poor tall child sat down and cried as if her heart would break.

So she cried, and she cried. And her tears ran down the middle of the hall, like a deep river. And very soon there was quite a large Pool of Tears, reaching halfway down the hall.

And there she might have stayed, till this very day, if the White Rabbit hadn't happened to come through the hall, on his way to visit the Duchess. He was dressed up as grand as grand could be, and he had a pair of white kid gloves in one hand, and a little fan in the other hand; and he kept on muttering to himself "Oh, the Duchess, the Duchess! Oh, *won't* she be savage if I've kept her waiting!"

But he didn't see Alice, you know. So, when she began to say "If you please, Sir—" her voice seemed to come from the top of the hall, because her head was so high up. And the Rabbit was so dreadfully frightened; and he dropped the gloves and the fan, and ran away as hard as he could go.

Then a *very* curious thing indeed happened. Alice took up the fan, and began to fan herself with it: and, lo and behold, she got quite small again, and, all in a minute, she was just about the size of a mouse!

Now look at the picture, and you'll soon guess what happened next. It looks just like the sea, doesn't it? But it *really* is the Pool of Tears—all made of *Alice's* tears, you know!

And Alice has tumbled into the Pool; and the Mouse has tumbled in; and there they are, swimming about together.

Doesn't Alice look so very pretty, as she swims across the picture? You can just see

her blue stockings, deep under the water.

But why is the Mouse swimming away from Alice in such a hurry? Well, the reason is that Alice began talking about cats and dogs; and a Mouse always *hates* talking about cats and dogs!

Suppose *you* were swimming about, in a Pool of your own Tears; and suppose somebody began talking to *you* about lesson-books and bottles of medicine, wouldn't *you* swim away as hard as you could go?

4. *THE CAUCUS-RACE*

When Alice and the Mouse had got out of the Pool of Tears, of course they were very wet; and so were a lot of other curious creatures that had tumbled in as well. There was a Dodo (that's the great bird, in front, leaning on a walking-stick); and a Duck; and a Lory (that's just behind the Duck, looking over its head); and an Eaglet (that's on the left-hand side of the Lory); and several others.

Well, and so they didn't know how in the world they were to get dry again. But the Dodo—who was a very wise bird—told them the right way was to have a Caucus-Race. And what do you think *that* was?

You don't know? Well, you *are* an ignorant child! Now, be very attentive, and I'll soon cure you of your ignorance!

First, you must have a *race-course*. It ought to be a *sort* of circle, but it doesn't much matter *what* shape it is, so long as it goes a good way round, and joins on to itself again.

Then, you must put all the *racers* on the course, here and there; it doesn't matter *where,* so long as you don't crowd them too much together.

Then, you needn't say "One, two, three, and away!" but let them all set off running just when they like, and leave off just when they like.

So all of these creatures, Alice and all, went on running round and round, till they were all quite dry again. And then the Dodo said *everybody* had won, and *everybody* must have prizes!

Of course *Alice* had to give them their prizes. And she had nothing to give them but a few sweets she happened to have in her pocket. And there was just one sweet a-piece, all round. And there was no prize at all for Alice!

So what do you think they did? Alice had nothing left but her thimble. Now take a look at the picture, and you'll see what happened.

"Hand it over here!" said the Dodo.

Then the Dodo took the thimble and handed it back to Alice, and said "We beg your acceptance of this elegant thimble!" And then all the other creatures cheered.

Wasn't *that* a curious sort of present to give her? Suppose they wanted to give *you* a birthday present, would you rather they should go to your toy cupboard, and pick out your nicest doll, and say "Here, my love, here's a lovely birthday present for you!" or would you like them to give you something *new,* something that *didn't* belong to you before?

5. BILL, THE LIZARD

Now I'm going to tell you about Alice's Adventures in the White Rabbit's house.

Do you remember how the Rabbit dropped his gloves and his fan, when he was so frightened at hearing Alice's voice, that seemed to come down from the sky? Well, of course he couldn't go to visit the Duchess *without* his gloves and his fan; so, after a bit, he came back again to look for them.

By this time the Dodo and all the other curious creatures had gone away, and Alice was wandering about all alone.

So what do you think he did? Actually he thought she was his housemaid, and began ordering her about! "Mary Ann!" said the Rabbit. "Go home this very minute, and fetch me a pair of gloves and a fan! Quick, now!"

Perhaps he couldn't see very clearly with his pink eyes, for I'm sure Alice doesn't look very much *like* a housemaid, *does* she? However, she was a very good-natured little girl, so she wasn't a bit offended, but ran off to the Rabbit's house as quickly as she could.

It was lucky she found the door open: for, if she had had to ring, I suppose the *real* Mary Ann would have come to open the door; and she would *never* have let Alice come in. And I'm sure it was *very* lucky she didn't meet the real Mary Ann, as she trotted upstairs; for I'm afraid she would have taken Alice for a robber!

So at last she found her way into the Rabbit's room; and there was a pair of gloves lying on the table, and she was just going to take them up and go away when she happened to see a little bottle on the table. And of course it had the words "DRINK ME!" on the label. And of course Alice drank some!

Well, I think that was *rather* lucky, too, don't *you?* For, if she *hadn't* drunk any, all this wonderful adventure that I'm going to tell you about would not have happened at all. And wouldn't *that* have been a pity?

You're getting so used to Alice's adventures that I daresay you can guess what happened next? If you can't, then I'll tell you.

She grew, and she grew, and she grew. And in a very short time the room was full of *Alice:* in the same way as a jar is full of jam! There was *Alice* all the way up to the ceiling; and *Alice* in every corner of the room!

The door opened inwards; so of course there wasn't any room to open it, so when the Rabbit got tired of waiting and came to fetch his gloves for himself, of course he couldn't get in.

So what do you think he did? (Now we come to the picture.)

He sent Bill, the Lizard, up to the roof of the house, and told him to get down the chimney. But Alice happened to have one of her feet in the fireplace; so, when she heard Bill coming down the chimney, she just gave a little tiny kick, and away went Bill, flying up into the sky!

Poor little Bill! Don't you pity him so very much? How frightened that Lizard must have been!

6. THE DEAR LITTLE PUPPY

Well, it doesn't look such a very little Puppy, does it? But then, you see, Alice had grown very small indeed; and that's what makes the Puppy look so large. When Alice had eaten one of those little magic cakes that she found in the White Rabbit's house, it made her get quite small, directly, so that she could get through the door; or else she could never have got out of the house again. Wouldn't that have been a pity? Because then she wouldn't have dreamed all the other curious things that we're going to read about.

So it really *was* a *little* Puppy, you see. And isn't it a little *pet*? And look at the way it's barking at the little stick that Alice is holding out for it! You can see she was just a *little* afraid of it, all the time, because she's standing behind that great thistle, for fear the Puppy should run over her. That would have been just about as bad, for *her*, as it would be for *you* to be run over by a waggon and four horses!

Have you got a little pet puppy at *your* home? If you have, I hope you're always kind to it, and give it nice things to eat.

Once upon a time, I knew some little children, about as big as you; and they had a little pet dog of their own; and it was called *Dash*. And this is what they told me about its birthday treat.

"Do you know, one day we remembered it was Dash's birthday that day. So we said 'Let's give Dash a nice birthday treat, like what we have on *our* birthdays!' So we thought and we thought 'Now, what is it *we* like best of all, on *our* birthdays?' And we thought and we thought. And at last we all called out together 'Why, it's *oatmeal porridge*, of course!' So naturally we thought Dash would be *quite* sure to like porridge very much, too.

"So we went to the cook, and we got her to make a saucerful of nice oatmeal porridge. And then we called Dash into the house, and we said 'Now, Dash, you're going to have your birthday treat!' We expected Dash would jump for joy: but it didn't, one bit!

"So we put the saucer down before it, and we said 'Now, Dash, don't be greedy! Eat it nicely, like a good dog!'

"So Dash just tasted it with the tip of its tongue: and then it made, oh, such a horrid face! And then, do you know, it did *hate* it so, it wouldn't eat a bit more of it! So we had to put it all down its throat with a spoon!"

I wonder if Alice will give *this* little Puppy some porridge? I don't think she *can*, because she hasn't got any with her. I can't see any saucer in the picture.

7. THE BLUE CATERPILLAR

Would you like to know what happened to Alice, after she had got away from the Puppy? It was far too large an animal, you know, for *her* to play with. (I don't suppose *you* would much enjoy playing with a young Hippopotamus, would you? You would always be expecting to be crushed as flat as a pancake under its great heavy feet!) So Alice was very glad to run away, while it wasn't looking.

Well, she wandered up and down, and didn't know what in the world to do, to make herself grow back up to her right size again. Of course she knew that she had to eat or drink *something*: that was the regular rule, you know: but she couldn't guess *what* thing.

However, she soon came to a great big mushroom that was so tall that she couldn't see over the top of it without standing on tip-toe. And what do you think she saw? Something that I'm sure *you* have never talked to, in all your life!

It was a very large Blue Caterpillar.

I'll tell you, soon, what Alice and the Caterpillar talked about; but first let us have a good look at the picture.

That curious thing you can see standing in front of the Caterpillar is called a "hookah"; and it's used for smoking. The smoke comes through that long tube, that winds round and round like a serpent.

And do you see the caterpillar's long nose and chin? At least, they *look* exactly like a nose and chin, don't they? But they really *are* two of its legs. You know a Caterpillar has got *quantities* of legs; you can see some more of them, further down.

What a real bother it must be to a Caterpillar, counting over such a lot of legs, every night, to make sure it hasn't lost any of them!

And *another* great bother must be having to settle *which* leg it had better move first. I think, if *you* had forty or fifty legs, and if you wanted to go for a walk, you'd be such a time in settling which leg to begin with that you'd never go for a walk at all!

And what did Alice and the Caterpillar *talk* about, I wonder?

Well, Alice told it how *very* confusing it was, being first one size and then another.

And the Caterpillar asked her if she liked the size she was, just then.

And Alice said she would like to be just a *little* bit larger—three inches was such a *wretched* height to be! (Just mark off three inches on the wall, about the length of your middle finger, and you'll see what size poor Alice was.)

And the Caterpillar told her one side of the mushroom would make her grow *taller,* and the other side would make her grow *shorter.*

So Alice took two little bits of it with her to nibble, and managed to make herself quite a nice comfortable height, before she went on to visit the Duchess.

8. THE PIG-BABY

Would you like to hear all about Alice's visit to the Duchess? It was a very interesting visit indeed, I can assure you.

Of course, she knocked at the door to begin with; but nobody came so she had to open the door for herself.

Now, if you look at the picture, you'll see just exactly what Alice saw when she got inside.

The door led right into the kitchen, you see. The Duchess sat in the middle of the room, nursing the Baby. The Baby was howling. The soup was boiling. The Cook was stirring the soup. The Cat—it was a *Cheshire*-Cat—was grinning, as Cheshire-Cats always do. All these things were happening just as Alice went in.

The Duchess has a beautiful cap and gown, hasn't she? But I'm afraid she *hasn't* got a very beautiful *face.*

The Baby—well, I daresay you've seen *several* nicer babies than *that;* and more good-tempered ones, too. However, take a good look at it, and we'll see if you know it again next time you meet it!

The Cook—well, you *may* have seen nicer cooks, once or twice.

But I'm nearly sure you've *never* seen a nicer *Cat!* Now *have* you? And *wouldn't* you like to have a Cat of your own, just like that one, with lovely green eyes, and smiling so sweetly?

The Duchess was very rude to Alice. And no wonder. Why, she even called her own *Baby* "Pig!" And it *wasn't* a Pig, *was*

it? And she ordered the Cook to chop off Alice's head; though of course the Cook didn't do it. And at last she threw the Baby at her! Alice caught the Baby, and took it away with her; and I think that was the best thing Alice could do.

So she wandered away, through the wood, carrying the ugly little thing with her. And a great job it was to keep hold of it, it wriggled about so. But at last she found out that the *proper* way was to keep tight hold of its left foot and its right ear.

But don't *you* try to hold a Baby like that, my Child! There are not many babies who would *like* being nursed in *that* way!

Well, and so the Baby kept grunting, and grunting, so that Alice had to say to it, quite seriously, "If you're going to turn into a *Pig*, my dear, I'll have nothing more to do with you. Mind now!"

And at last she looked down into its face, and what *do* you think had happened to it? Look at the picture, and see if you can guess.

"Why, *that's* not the Baby that Alice was nursing, is it?"

Ah, I *knew* you wouldn't know it again, though I told you to take a good look at it! Yes, it *is* the Baby. And it's turned into a little *Pig!*

So Alice put it down, and let it trot away into the wood. And she said to herself "It was a *very* ugly *Baby;* but it makes rather a handsome *Pig,* I think."

Don't you think she was right?

9. THE CHESHIRE-CAT

All alone, all alone! Poor Alice! No Baby, not even a *Pig* to keep her company!

So you may be sure she was very glad indeed when she saw the Cheshire-Cat, perched up in a tree, over her head.

The Cat has a very nice smile, no doubt: but just look and see what a lot of teeth it's got! Isn't Alice just a *little* shy of the Cat?

Well, yes, a *little.* But then, it couldn't help having teeth, you know; and it *could* have helped smiling, supposing it had been cross. So, on the whole, she was *glad.*

Doesn't Alice look very prim, holding her head so straight up, and with her hands behind her, just as if she were going to say her lessons to the Cat!

And that reminds me. There's a little lesson I want to teach *you*, while we're looking at this picture of Alice and the Cat. Now don't be in a bad temper about it, my dear Child! It's a very *little* lesson indeed!

Do you see that Fox-Glove growing close to the tree? And do you know why it's called a *Fox*-Glove? Perhaps you think it's got something to do with a Fox? No indeed! *Foxes* never wear Gloves!

The right word is "*Folk's*-Gloves". Did you ever hear that Fairies used to be called "the good *Folk*"?

Now we've finished the lesson, and we'll wait a minute, till you've got your temper again.

Well? Do you feel quite good-natured again? No temper-ache? No crossness about the corners of the mouth? Then we'll go on.

"Cheshire Puss!" said Alice. (*Wasn't* that a pretty name for a Cat?) "Would you kindly tell me which way I ought to go from here?"

And so the Cheshire-Cat told her which way she ought to go if she wanted to visit the Hatter, and which way to go to visit the March Hare. "They're both mad!" warned the Cat.

And then the Cat vanished away, just like the flame of a candle when it goes out!

So Alice set off to visit the March Hare. And as she went along, there was the Cat again! And she told it plainly she didn't *like* it coming and going so quickly.

So this time the Cat vanished quite slowly, beginning with the tail, and ending with the grin. Wasn't *that* a curious thing, a Grin without any Cat?

10. THE MAD TEA-PARTY

If you turn the page you'll see the Mad Tea-Party. You see Alice had left the Cheshire-Cat and gone to see the March Hare and the Hatter, as the Cheshire-Cat had advised her. She found them having tea under a tree, with a Dormouse sitting between them.

There were only those three at the table, but there were quantities of teacups set all along it. You can't see all of the table, you know, and even in the bit you *can* see there are nine cups, counting the one the March Hare has got in his hand.

That's the March Hare, with the long ears, and straws mixed up with his hair. The straws showed he was mad—I don't know why. Never twist up straws among *your* hair, for fear people should think you're mad!

There was a nice green armchair at the end of the table, that looked as if it was just meant for Alice; so she went over and sat down in it.

Then she had quite a long talk with the March Hare and the Hatter. The Dormouse didn't say much. You see it was fast asleep generally, and it only just woke up for a moment, now and then.

As long as it was asleep, it was very useful to the March Hare and the Hatter, because it had a nice round soft head, just

to sell; and even the one that he's got on his head is meant to be sold. You see it's got its price marked on it—a "10" and a "6"—that means "ten shillings and sixpence". Wasn't that a funny way of selling hats? And hasn't he got a beautiful neck-tie on? Such a lovely yellow tie, with large red spots.

He has just got up to say to Alice "Your hair wants cutting!" That was a rude thing to say, *wasn't* it? And do you think her hair *does* want cutting? *I* think it's actually a very pretty length—just the right length in fact.

11. THE QUEEN'S GARDEN

This is a little bit of the beautiful garden I told you about. You see Alice had managed at last to get quite small, so that she could go through the little door. I suppose she was about as tall as a mouse, if it stood on its hind-legs; so of course this was a *very* tiny rose-tree, and these are *extremely* tiny gardeners.

What funny little men they are! But *are* they men, do you think? I think they must be live cards, with just a head, and arms, and legs, so as to *look* like little men. And what *are* they doing with that red paint, I wonder? Well, you see, this is what they told Alice. The Queen of Hearts wanted to have a *red* rose-tree just in that corner: and these poor little gardeners had made a great mistake, and had put in a *white* one

like a pillow; so they could put their elbows on it, and lean across it, and talk to each other quite comfortably. You wouldn't like people to use *your* head for a pillow, *would* you? But if you were fast asleep, like the Dormouse, you wouldn't feel it; so I suppose you wouldn't care about it.

I'm afraid they gave Alice *very* little to eat and drink. However, after a bit, she helped herself to some tea and bread-and-butter; only I don't quite see where she *got* the bread-and-butter, and she had no plate for it. Nobody seems to have a plate except the Hatter. I do believe the March Hare must have had one as well because, when they all moved one place on (that was the rule at this curious tea-party), and Alice had to go into the place of the March Hare, she found he had just upset the milk jug into his plate. So I suppose his plate and the milk jug are hidden behind that large teapot.

The Hatter once carried about with him hats

instead. And they were so frightened about it, because the Queen was *sure* to be angry, and then she would order all their heads to be cut off!

She was a dreadfully savage Queen, and that was what she always did, when she was angry with people. "Off with their heads!" You know, they didn't *really* cut their heads off because nobody ever did obey her; but that was what she always *said*.

Now can't you guess what those poor little gardeners are trying to do? They're trying to paint the roses *red*, and they're in a great hurry to get it done before the Queen comes. And then *perhaps* the Queen won't find out it was a *white* rose-tree to begin with: and then *perhaps* the little men won't get their heads cut off!

You see there were *five* large white roses on the tree—such a job to get them all painted red! But they've got three and a half done, now, and if only they wouldn't stop to talk—work away, little men, oh, *do* work away! Or the Queen will be coming before it's done! And if she finds any *white* roses on the tree, do you know what will happen? It will be "Off with their heads!" Oh, work away, my little men! Hurry, hurry!

The Queen has come! And *isn't* she angry? Oh, my poor little Alice!

12. THE LOBSTER-QUADRILLE

Did you ever play Croquet? There are large wooden balls, painted with different colors, that you have to roll about; and arches of wire, that you have to send them through; and great wooden mallets, with long handles, to knock the balls about with.

Now look at the picture, and you'll see that *Alice* has just been playing a Game of Croquet.

"But she *couldn't* play, with that great red what's-its-name in her arms! Why, how could she hold the mallet?"

Well! Do you know *anything?* That's the question. However, look at the picture. That creature with a red head, and red claws, and green scales, is the *Gryphon.* Now you know.

And the other's the *Mock Turtle.* It's got a calf's-head, because calf's-head is used to make *Mock Turtle Soup.* Now you know.

"But what are they *doing,* going round and round Alice like that?"

Why, I thought of *course* you'd know *that!* They're dancing *a Lobster-Quadrille.*

And next time *you* meet a Gryphon and a Mock Turtle, I daresay they'll dance it for *you,* if you ask them prettily. Only don't let them come *so* close, or they'll be treading on your toes, as they did on poor Alice's.

13. WHO STOLE THE TARTS?

Did you ever hear how the Queen of Hearts made some tarts? And can you tell me what became of them?

"Why, of *course* I can! Doesn't the song tell all about it?

The Queen of Hearts, she made
   some tarts,
All on a summer day:
The Knave of Hearts, he stole
   those tarts,
And took them quite away!"

Well, yes, the *song* says so. But it would never do to punish the poor Knave, just because there was a little *song* about him. They had to take him prisoner, and put chains on his wrists, and bring him before the King of Hearts, so that there might be a regular trial.

Now, if you look at the picture you'll see what a grand thing a trial is, when the Judge is a King!

The King is very grand, *isn't* he? But he doesn't look very *happy.* I do believe that

Why, my dear Child, that great red what's-its-name (its *real* name is *"a Flamingo"*) *is* the mallet! In this Croquet-Game, the balls were live *Hedgehogs*—you know a hedgehog can roll itself up into a ball?—and the mallets were live *Flamingos!*

So Alice is just resting from the game, for a minute, to have a chat with that dear old thing, the Duchess; and of course she keeps her mallet under her arm, so as not to lose it.

"But I don't think she *was* a dear old thing, one bit! To call her Baby a *Pig,* and to want to chop off Alice's head!"

Oh, that was only a joke, about chopping off Alice's head; and as to the Baby—why, it *was* a Pig, you know! And just look at her *smile!* Why, it's wider than all of Alice's head; and yet you can only see half of it!

Well, they'd only had a *very* little chat, when the Queen came and took Alice away, to see the Gryphon and the Mock Turtle.

You don't know what a Gryphon is?

big crown, on the top of his wig, must be *extremely* heavy and uncomfortable. But he had to wear them *both,* you see, so that people might know he was a Judge *as well as* a King.

And *doesn't* the Queen look cross? She can see the dish of tarts on the table, that she had taken such trouble to make. And she can see the bad Knave (do you see the chains hanging from his wrists?) that stole them away from her; so I don't think it's any wonder if she *does* feel a *little* cross.

The White Rabbit is standing near the King, reading out the song, to tell everybody what a bad Knave he is: and the Jury (you can just see two of them, up in the Jury-box, the Frog and the Duck) have to decide whether he's "guilty" or "not guilty".

Now I'll tell you about the accident that happened to Alice.

You see, she was sitting close by the Jury-box: and she was called as a witness. Do you know what a "witness" is? Well, a "witness" is a person who has seen the prisoner do whatever he's accused of, or at any rate knows *something* that's important in the trial.

But *Alice* hadn't seen the Queen *make* the tarts; and she hadn't seen the Knave *take* the tarts. And, in fact, she didn't know anything about it: so why in the world they wanted *her* to be a witness, I'm sure *I* can't tell you!

Anyhow, they *did* want her. And the White Rabbit blew his big trumpet, and shouted out "Alice!" And so Alice jumped up in a great hurry. And then—

And then what *do* you think happened? Why, her skirt caught against the Jury-box, and tipped it over, and all the poor little Jurors came tumbling out of it!

Now let's try and see if we can make out all the twelve. You know there ought to be twelve to make up a Jury. I see the Frog, and the Dormouse, and the Rat and the Ferret; and I can see the Hedgehog, and the Lizard, and the Bantam-Cock, and the Mole, and the Duck, and the Squirrel, and a screaming bird, with a long beak, just behind the Mole.

But that only makes eleven: we must find one more creature.

Oh, do you see a little white head, coming out behind the Mole, and just under the Duck's beak? That makes up the twelve.

The screaming bird is a *Storkling* (of course you know what *that* is?) and the little white head is a *Mouseling.* Isn't it a little *darling*?

Alice picked them all up again, very carefully, and I hope they weren't *much* hurt!

14. THE SHOWER OF CARDS

Oh dear, oh dear! What *is* it all about? And what's happening to Alice?

Well now, I'll tell you all about it, as well as I can. The way the trial ended was this. The King wanted the Jury to settle whether the Knave of Hearts was *guilty* or *not guilty*—that means that they were to settle whether *he* had stolen the Tarts, or if somebody else had in fact taken them. But the wicked *Queen* wanted to have his *punishment* settled, first of all. That wasn't at all fair, *was* it? Because, you know, supposing he never *took* the Tarts, then of course he oughtn't to be punished. Would *you* like to be punished for something you hadn't done?

So Alice said "Stuff and nonsense!"

So the Queen said "Off with her head!" (Just what she always said, when she was angry.)

So Alice replied "Who cares for *you*? You're nothing but a pack of cards!"

So they were *all* very angry, and flew up into the air: then they all came tumbling down again, all over poor Alice, just like a shower of rain.

And I think you'll *never* guess what happened next. The next thing was, Alice woke up out of her curious dream. And she found that the cards were only some leaves off the tree, that the wind had blown down upon her face.

Wouldn't it be a nice thing to have a curious dream, just like Alice?

The best plan is this. First lie down under a tree, and wait till a White Rabbit runs by, with a watch in its hand: then shut your eyes tight, and pretend that you are dear little Alice.

Goodbye, Alice dear, goodbye!

Gulliver's Travels

Swift, edited by Marie-Louise Taylor

GULLIVER'S VOYAGE TO LILLIPUT

During my voyage from the South Seas to the East Indies we were driven by a violent storm to the northwest of Van Diemen's Land, and shipwrecked. What became of my companions I cannot tell, but I suppose they were all drowned. I swam as strongly as I could, and just when I was almost finished, I found myself within my depth, and I could walk to the shore. I arrived about eight o'clock in the evening, but could not discern any signs of inhabitants; and being very tired, I lay down on the short grass and fell asleep. I slept for nine hours, and sounder than I ever had done in my life.

When I woke up it was daylight, and I at once tried to get up; but to my astonishment I found my arms and legs had been strongly fastened to the ground, as well as my long thick hair, while numerous slender cords were passed across my body. I was lying on my back, and therefore I could only look upwards to the sun, which soon became very painful to my eyes. I heard a confused noise, but could see nothing; but presently I felt something moving up my left leg, then over my stomach, and almost up to my chin. By bending my eyes downwards I saw it was a human creature not six inches high, with a bow and arrow in his hands and a quiver at his back—forty more of the very same kind following him. When they had ventured as far as to get a full view of my face, he lifted up his hands and eyes by way of admiration, and cried out in a shrill but distinct voice, "Hekinah degul"—the others repeating those same words several times.

Struggling to free myself I broke the strings and wrenched out the pegs that fastened my left arm to the ground; whereupon there was a great shrill shout, and in an instant I felt about a hundred arrows discharged on my left hand, which pricked me like so many needles. They then fired another volley into the air, some falling on my face, causing great pain; so I thought the most prudent thing to do was to be still till night, when I could easily free myself.

When the people saw I was quiet they fired no more arrows; and then began a knocking over against my right ear like people at work. By turning my head that way as well as I could, I saw that they were erecting a stage about a foot and a half from the ground, large enough to hold four of the inhabitants. When they had climbed up by help of the ladders, one of them, who seemed to be a person of quality, ordered the strings to be cut that fastened the left side of my head. This gave me liberty to turn to the right, so that I could observe him while he made his long speech. He appeared to be of middle age, and taller than the other three who attended him. I understood him by his manner—while he spoke he used threats, showed symptoms of pity, and gave promises of kindness, to all of which I answered in a most submissive manner. Being very hungry, I put my finger to my mouth to signify that I required food, and I was glad to find the Hurgo or great lord understood me very well.

He descended from the stage and gave his orders, when about a hundred of the inhabitants climbed and walked towards my mouth laden with baskets of food that

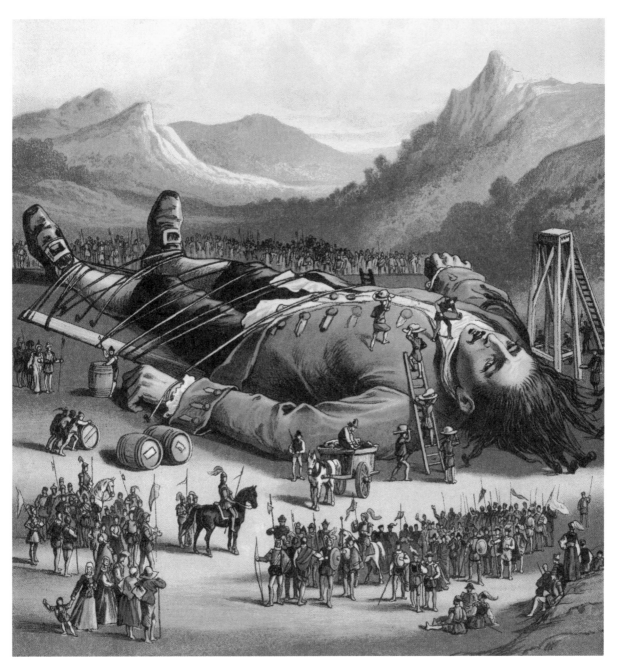

contained shoulders and legs of meat shaped like those of mutton, but smaller than the wings of a lark. These I ate by two or three at a mouthful, with three tiny loaves of bread at a time. They were filled with wonder and astonishment at my great appetite, and shouted for joy and danced on me after I had drunk up the contents of two of their largest hogsheads. When my appetite was appeased, there appeared a person of high rank from his Imperial Majesty with a message that I was to be conveyed as a prisoner to the capital city, but that I should be treated kindly. I then fell asleep, and slept for about eight hours.

Five hundred carpenters and engineers had been set to work to prepare the largest vehicle they had. It was a frame of wood raised three inches from the ground, about seven feet long and four wide, moving on twenty-two wheels, and drawn by fifteen hundred of the Emperor's largest horses, each about four and a half inches high. The great difficulty was to raise and place me on this vehicle. Eighty poles, each one foot high, were erected for this purpose, and by the help of extremely thin cords fastened to hooks in the bandages the workmen rolled round me, I was drawn up by nine hundred of the strongest men by these cords passed through pulleys in the poles. In three hours this was done, and I was flung into the vehicle and there tied fast. All this they did to me while I slept profoundly.

We made a long march and rested at night, with five hundred guards on each side of me, half with torches and half with bows and arrows, ready to shoot me if I should stir. The distance to the city was one mile, and by rising at sunrise we reached within two hundred yards of the city gates about noon. The Emperor and all his court then came out to meet us; but though he wished to do it, the great officers of state would not allow His Majesty to endanger his person by climbing on my body.

The largest building in the whole kingdom was an ancient temple now unused, and the vehicle on which I lay was drawn up in front of it. Here I was held down by ninety-one chains fastened to the temple, and locked to my ankles with thirty-six padlocks. Being now secure, they cut all the strings that bound me; and when I rose up and walked backwards and forwards as far as my chains would permit, it is impossible to find words to express the astonishment of the people. The great gate of the temple was about four feet high and two broad, and I was able to lie down at my full length in it if it so pleased me.

Standing on my feet I looked about me, and saw that the fields resembled beds of flowers, and the tallest trees appeared to be about seven feet high. I must confess I never beheld a more entertaining prospect. The Emperor and his court had been viewing me from a turret at least five feet high, over against the temple. He now descended and advanced towards me on horseback, but the beast reared at the sight of me. Thanks to the Emperor's good horsemanship, he managed to keep his seat till the attendants ran in and held the bridle.

He is taller than any of his subjects, which was enough to strike awe into the hearts of his people. His features are strong and masculine, his deportment majestic, and all his motions graceful. His dress was very plain and simple, but he had on his head a light helmet of gold, set with jewels, and adorned with a plume and crest. He held his sword in his hand, to defend himself if need be. It was three inches long, the hilt and scabbard of gold enriched with diamonds. The ladies and courtiers were all most magnificently clad, so that the spot they stood on seemed to resemble a petticoat spread on the ground embroidered with figures of gold and silver. His Supreme Majesty spoke often to me, and I returned answers; but neither of us could understand a syllable. After about two hours the court retired, and I was left with a strong guard to keep off the rabble, who now crowded round me.

I was a source of great concern to the Emperor and his court. They did not know what to do with me. They feared I would break loose—that my appetite might cause a famine; but when they thought they had better kill me, they remembered how difficult it would be to bury such a huge carcass. Hearing from the officers of my guard that I was very good-natured, an imperial commission was sent out obliging all the villages round the city to deliver food and drink for me every morning. Six hundred persons were set apart to be my servants; three hundred tailors were employed to make me a suit after the fashion of the country; and six of His Majesty's greatest scholars were employed to instruct me in their language. In three weeks' time I had made great progress in learning their language, so that I was able to converse with the Emperor quite freely.

One day he asked if I would agree to be searched, for no doubt I might carry about several weapons, which must be dangerous things. I agreed to this, saying I was ready to strip myself and turn out my pockets before him. He replied that, by the laws of the country, I must be searched by two of his officers, but he could trust these persons in my hands. I then took up the two officers and put them first into my coat pockets, and then into every other pocket about me, except my two fobs, in one of which there was a silver watch, and in the other a small quantity of gold in a purse. The gentlemen, having pen, ink and some paper about them, made an exact inventory of all the articles they found, and then asking to be set down, they delivered it to the Emperor. In the left pocket they came upon my snuff-box, and being unable to lift it, I took it out. They then asked me to open it, which I did, when they both stepped into it; and the snuff flying up into their faces

set them sneezing several times. I need not say how very much surprised they were at all the articles, more especially a comb, which they described as "a sort of engine, from the back of which were extended twenty long poles," with which "they supposed the *man-mountain* combs his head". When the inventory was read over to the Emperor, he directed me to deliver up my sword, and next one of the hollow iron pillars, by which he meant my pocket-pistols. I delivered up the pistols, with my pouch of powder and bullets, asking them to be very careful with the powder, as it would kindle with the slightest spark and blow up his imperial palace into the air. I likewise gave over to two of the tallest yeomen of the guard my watch, which they bore on a pole

on their shoulders. I then gave up my silver and copper money, my purse containing some gold pieces, my knife and razor, my comb and silver snuff-box, my handkerchief and journal-book.

Though they loaded me with marks of kindness, I greatly desired my liberty, and petitioned many times for it. At last it was granted on certain conditions; namely, that I should serve the Emperor and help his subjects in various ways. My chains were then unlocked, and I was free, the Emperor doing me the honor to appear in person during the entire ceremony. After many kind words he said he hoped I should prove a useful servant.

One morning there came to my house a messenger from the Emperor, and standing on my hand he told me we were threatened

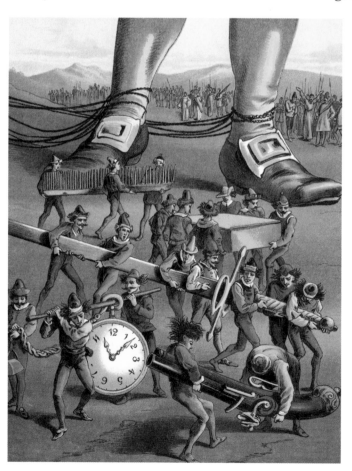

by a quarrel at home and an invasion from abroad. The quarrel at home was something about wearing high or low heels, and cutting off the narrow end of eggs instead of the broad. As I was the subject of different country, I refused to mix myself up with this quarrel, but sent my respects to the Emperor, and let him know that I was ready, with the hazard of my life, to defend his person and state against the foreign enemy, who was coming against him with a great fleet. This I was able to do by what they were pleased to consider an extraordinary strategy; namely, that I caused several of their largest cables to be handed over to me, as well as some bars of iron. Wading off with them to the harbor of the enemy, I fastened the chains securely to fifty of their largest ships, and drew them after me in spite of the arrows that were fired at me, many of them taking effect in my face and causing much pain. I was very fortunate in taking them all safe to the royal port of Lilliput, where I was made a *nardac* upon the spot, which is the highest honor among them.

This success made the Emperor ambitious to take his enemy completely, and make slaves of them. I therefore was requested to bring the whole of the enemy's ships into port; but this I stoutly refused to do, whereupon the Emperor could never forgive me, and he and some of his nobles were quite set against me. I, however, was able to render numerous valuable services to the Emperor that were great in their eyes, though of no account in mine.

By now I had lived happy and contented for more than nine and a half months with them, and would no doubt have stayed longer had I not heard there was a design to accuse me of high treason, and that articles were drawn up against me, and an agreement come to put out both my eyes, as well as to slowly starve me to death. So I made my escape to the nearby kingdom of Blefuscu, and was given a grand reception.

Just three days after my arrival in Blefuscu, while walking along the coast, I observed a large object floating in the sea. I waded in, and imagine my delight to find a real boat turned upside down. With the assistance of twenty of the largest vessels the King had kindly lent to me, as well as two thousand men armed with ropes and engines, I turned the boat up, and found that it was damaged only slightly. I received from the King the materials to fit it up, together with the liberty to depart.

In the meantime the Emperor of Lilliput sent for me to return, but his ambassador was informed I had found a vessel able to carry me to sea, that I was now storing it, preparing for a start immediately. The vessel was carefully searched to see if no-one had stowed himself away. I then set sail, and arrived in the Downs after a most prosperous voyage, almost a year later.

GULLIVER'S VOYAGE TO BROBDINGNAG

Two months after my return from Lilliput I went to sea again, in the ship *Adventure*, and had a prosperous voyage till we arrived at the Cape of Good Hope, where we landed for a fresh supply of water. After we set sail again there was a very great storm that carried us far to the east. To our delight a boy on the topmast discovered land, which proved to be either a large island or a continent; and being again short of water, we anchored. The captain sent a dozen men ashore, well armed, in search of water. I got permission to go with them, but when the men went towards the east to look for a river or spring, I turned westward and walked about a mile alone through barren and rocky country. When I was weary I returned to the creek; but to my horror I found the men were not only in the boat, but were rowing for their lives to the ship, followed by a huge creature walking into the sea after them as fast as it could. Luckily, the sea was full of sharp-pointed rocks, so that the monster, in spite of the great strides it was able to take, could not overtake them.

I made off as fast as I could, climbed up a steep hill where I could look about me, and was very much surprised to find the ground well cultivated, with hay standing twenty feet high, and the corn forty at least. I found my way onto a path through a field

of barley, and came to a stile; but the steps were each six feet high, so I could not climb over it. I was trying to find a gap in the hedge, when I saw one of the inhabitants in the next field coming to the stile. He was as tall as an ordinary church steeple; and as I was much afraid of him, I hid myself in the corn. When on my side of the stile, the giant looked back, and calling out in a very loud voice, seven monsters as huge as himself came towards him carrying enormous reaping-hooks in their hands and according to orders began to reap the barley in the field where I lay. I kept away from them at as great a distance as I could, but at last was so worn out that I lay down between two ridges.

Soon after, one of the reapers came so close to me that I was afraid at the next step he would squash me to death under his foot, or cut me in two with his hook; so I screamed out as loud as I could, when the giant monster began to look about him on the ground, and spied me. After looking at me for a while he at last ventured to take me up by the middle between his thumb and forefinger, and brought me close to his eyes. I was afraid he would dash me down; but being pleased with my voice and my gestures, he began to look upon me as a curiosity. Lifting up the lapel of his coat he put me into it, and ran off to his master with me. At first he took me for a strange animal; but when he saw I walked erect like himself, he and his seven servants sat down round me, the better to watch my movements. He seemed to come to the conclusion I was indeed a man.

Sending his servants to their work, he wrapped me up in his pocket-handkerchief and carried me off to his house. When he showed me to his wife, she screamed as if she had seen a toad or a spider; but when she saw my polite bows and signs of friendship, she became quite kind to me.

A servant now brought in dinner; and when the family were sat down, the farmer placed me on the table, which was thirty feet from the floor. His wife minced a bit of meat and crumbled some bread for me; for which I made her a low bow, took out my knife and fork, and began to eat, to their great delight.

In the midst of dinner the mistress's cat leaped into her lap—a creature three times as large as a cow. At first I was very much afraid, but showing a bold face towards her, she held herself back as if afraid of me. I had less fear of the dogs that wandered into the room; though one—a mastiff—must have been equal in bulk to four elephants, and a gray bloodhound taller, though not so large.

When dinner was nearly done the nurse brought in the baby, about a year old, who at once spied me, and began to cry to get me for a plaything. The mother, out of pure indulgence, took me up, when the child at once caught me by the middle and stuffed my head into his mouth. I roared so loud that he became frightened and let me drop; and I should certainly have broken my neck, if the mother had not held her apron under me.

When dinner was finished my master returned to his labors, giving his wife strict charge to take care of me. I was very tired, and my mistress, seeing that I was sleepy, laid me in her own bed, covering me with a clean white handkerchief, which was larger than the sail of the largest ship. I slept very soundly, dreaming I was at home with my wife and children, which made it all the worse to wake up. Two rats about the size of a large mastiff now crept up the curtains, and one of them came very near to my face; whereupon I drew my sword to defend myself, and had the good fortune to kill one and wound the other severely. Soon after, my mistress came into the room, and seeing me all bloody, she took me in her hand, fearing I was hurt; but I pointed to the dead rat to show I was all right. One of the servants then threw the rat out of the window, while my mistress took me into the garden for a walk.

In the evening she and her nine-year-old daughter fitted up the baby's cradle for me. It was put into a drawer, and the drawer placed on a hanging shelf, for fear of the rats. Here I slept at night while I was with these people. This girl, my little nurse, was very good to me—sewing and washing my clothes, and teaching me the language, so that in a few days I could make my wants known. She called me Grildrig, which in English means mannikin.

My arrival soon began to be talked of, though they spoke of me as a strange animal who could speak a little language of my own, who had learned several words of theirs, who walked erect, was tame, gentle and obedient.

A dim-sighted farmer who lived nearby came to see me; he put on his spectacles to see me better, but his eyes looked so strange that I burst out laughing, and all the company did so too. This made the farmer very angry, and, being a miser, he advised my master to show me as a sight in the next town on market-day.

I guessed there was some mischief brewing against me when I observed my master and his friend whispering together; but the next morning Glumdalclitch, my dear little nurse, told me all. She was very sorry, fearing some rude, vulgar folks might squeeze me to death or break my bones. She said that her papa and mamma had promised that I, Grildrig, should be hers; but she found they meant to deceive her as they did last year, when they gave her a lamb, but when it was fat, sold it to a butcher.

My master took the advice of his friend, and carried me in a box to the nearest town next market-day. He took his daughter with him on a pillion behind. The box was closed on every side, with a door and holes bored for air; but with all the care my little nurse had shown in making it soft for me, I was terribly shaken in this journey, though it took only about half an hour. My master then alighted at an inn, and sent the crier round to say that a strange creature was to be seen at the sign of the Green Eagle, who could speak several words and perform a hundred diverting tricks. I was placed on a table, with my little nurse standing on a low stool to take care of me and tell me what to do. My master would only admit thirty people at a time so I was shown to twelve sets of company, and as often forced to act over again the same tricks, till I was half dead with weariness; for those who had seen me made such wonderful reports that the people were ready to break down the doors to come in.

I had no rest, for my master showed me in his own house to the neighboring gentlemen. It was only on a Wednesday, their Sabbath, that I was not shown.

He then made up his mind to set out for the metropolis, and also to show me in all the cities we passed through. Glumdalclitch carried me in her lap, in a box lined on all sides with the softest cloth she could get; and to get her father to take easy journeys, she complained she was tired with the trotting of the horse. She often took me out of the box to give me air and show me the country. We were ten weeks on our journey, during which I was shown in eighteen large towns and many villages, and to private families. Owing to the constant fatigue, I was almost reduced to a skeleton.

Still my master was determined to make the most out of me, though he thought I was dying. It was then that he was commanded to take me to court for the diversion of the Queen and her ladies. They were delighted with me; and when I fell on my knees and begged the honor of kissing the

Queen's imperial foot, she graciously held out her little finger, and I, with the utmost respect, put the tip of it to my lips. She asked me about my country and travels, and whether I would be content to live at court. Hearing I belonged to my master, she asked if he would sell me for a fair price. This he was ready enough to do, as he did not expect me to live a month. When the thousand pieces of gold was paid, I humbly begged that my dear Glumdalclitch might be admitted into her service, as she understood how to take care of me. Her Majesty agreed to this, and the farmer's consent was easily gained.

The Queen took me in her hand and carried me to the King; and he was much surprised by my rational answers. He sent for three great scholars who examined me closely, but could not make out what I was; only they could not believe I was a dwarf, because I was so very much smaller than the Queen's dwarf—the smallest man known in the kingdom. I assured the King I came from a country of millions of men and women of my own stature, where animals, trees, houses were all in proportion; where I could defend myself and find sustenance, as any of His Majesty's subjects could do here. The three men smiled with contempt; but the King dismissed them, sent for the farmer, questioned him, and at last made up his mind that all I said was no doubt true.

A convenient apartment was provided for me at court, and more suitable clothes; and the Queen became so fond of my company that she could not dine without me. On Wednesday she took me with the royal children to dine in the King's apartments, where my table and chair were placed at his left hand. He took much pleasure in conversing with me about the manners and customs of my country, making very wise observations on all I said.

Treated so very kindly by the King and Queen, and with my devoted nurse beside me, I would have been content but for the Queen's dwarf, who angered and mortified me daily by his remarks upon my littleness.

One day at dinner he was so nettled at me calling him brother, that he took me up by the middle and let me drop into a large bowl of cream, then ran away as fast as he could. I might have drowned, as my nurse was not near me, and the Queen was in too great a fright to stretch out her hand. Being a good swimmer, I managed to keep afloat till Glumdalclitch took me out. She put me to bed, and the dwarf was whipped, and forced to drink up the entire bowl of cream. He lost the favor of the Queen, who gave him to a lady, and to my great satisfaction I saw him no more. He had played many tricks on me, such as stuffing me into a marrow bone, and frightening me to death by catching handfuls of flies and other stinging insects and letting them fly off under my nose, just to divert the Queen.

It would take days to describe this vast country—the beauty of the King's palace and metropolis, as well as the chief temple. Yes, I should have lived happy enough in that place if my littleness had not exposed me to so many troublesome accidents. Glumdalclitch sometimes took me out to the garden, and there I was nearly killed one day by a hailstone; then I was carried off by the gardener's dog; and once I broke my right shin against the shell of a snail.

I had always felt that I should some time regain my liberty. Though the favorite of a king and a queen, I longed to be back in my own country, where I could walk about without fear of being trod to death like a frog or a young puppy. I had now been two years in the kingdom, when the King and Queen made a journey to the southeast, taking me and my nurse with them; and they rested at a city close to the seaside. I longed to see the ocean, and as Glumdalclitch was ill, I pretended to be so too, and asked leave to take the fresh air of the sea with a page whom I was very fond of; but Glumdalclitch burst into tears at parting, as if she foreboded something was about to happen.

The boy took me in my box to the seashore, where he set me down, and saying I desired to sleep in my hammock, he wandered along the beach. I was suddenly awakened with a violent pull upon the ring at the top of my box, and raised very high into the air and borne forward with great speed. I then found myself falling down so fast that I almost lost my breath; and also that I had fallen into the sea, and that my box was floating. I was four hours thus when I heard a great shout, repeated three times, in the English tongue, giving me such joy, for I knew I was close to a ship.

The carpenter of the ship got me out; and the captain, seeing my weak condition, made me lie down on his own bed: when I awoke I told him my whole story; and as a proof of what I said being all true, I took out of my cabinet, which had been taken on board, my small collection of rarities, including a comb I had made of hairs from the King's head set into a paring of the Queen's nail, some needles and pins a foot long, and a ring given to me from the Queen off her own finger, which she placed round my neck for a collar.

The captain, being a worthy gentleman, believed my word; and after a pleasant voyage and hiring a horse and guide for five shillings (which I borrowed from the captain), I set out for my house in Redriff. As I went along, the smallness of everything made me think I was in Lilliput; and when I arrived at my house, I looked down on the servants as if they had been pygmies and I a giant, so that they thought I had lost my wits. But I and my family, when my eyes got used to them, came to a right understanding; only my wife declared I should never go to sea again with *her* will.

The Princess Nobody

Andrew Lang

I. THE PRINCESS NOBODY

Once upon a time, when Fairies were much more common than they are today, there lived a King and Queen. Their country was near Fairy Land and often the little Elves would cross the border, and come into the King's fields and gardens. The girl-fairies would swing out of the bells of the fuchsias, and loll on the leaves, and drink the little drops of dew that fell down the stems. Here you may see all the Fairies making themselves merry at a picnic on a fuchsia, and an ugly little Dwarf is climbing up the stalk.

The King and Queen of the country next to Fairy Land were very rich, and very fond of each other; but one thing made them unhappy. They had no child, neither boy nor girl, to sit on the throne when they were dead and gone. Often the Queen said she wished she had a child, even if it were no bigger than her thumb; and she hoped the Fairies might hear her and help her. But they never took any notice. One day, when the King had been counting out his money all day (the day when the tributes were paid in), he grew very tired. He took off his crown, and went into his garden. Then he looked all round his kingdom, and said, "Ah! I would give it all for a BABY!"

No sooner had the King said this, than he heard a little squeaking voice near his foot. "You shall have a lovely Baby, if you will give me what I ask."

The King looked down, and there was the funniest little Dwarf that ever was seen. He had a red cap like a flower. He had a big moustache, and a short beard that curled outwards. His cloak was red and his coat was green, and he rode on a green Frog. Many people would have been frightened, but the King was used to Fairies.

138

"You shall have a beautiful Baby, if you will give me what I ask," said the Dwarf again.

"I'll give you anything you like," said the King.

"Then promise to give me NIENTE," said the Dwarf.

"Certainly," said the King (who had not an idea what NIENTE meant). "And how will you take it?"

"I will take *it*," said the Dwarf, "in my own way, on my own day."

With that he set spurs to his Frog, which cleared the garden path at one bound, and he was soon lost among the flowers.

Well, next day, a dreadful war broke out between the Ghosts and the Giants, and the King had to set forth and fight on the side of his friends the Giants.

A long, long time he was away; nearly a year. At last he came back to his own country, and he heard all the church bells ringing merrily. "What *can* be the matter?" said the King, and hurried to his Palace, where all the Courtiers rushed and told him that the Queen had a BABY.

"A girl or a boy?" asks the King.

"A Princess, Your Majesty," replies the Nurse, with a low curtsey, correcting him.

Well, you may fancy how glad the King was, although he would have *preferred* a boy. "What have you called her?" he asked.

"Till Your Majesty's return, we thought it better not to christen the Princess," said the Nurse, "so we have called her by the Italian name for *Nothing*: NIENTE; the Princess Niente, Your Majesty."

When the King heard *that*, and remembered that he had promised to give NIENTE to the Dwarf, he hid his face in his hands and groaned. Nobody knew what he meant, or why he was sad, so he thought it best to keep it to himself. He went in and kissed the Queen, and comforted her, and looked at the BABY. Never was there a BABY so beautiful; she was like a Fairy's child, and so light, she could sit on a flower and not crush it. She had little wings on her back; and all the birds were fond of her. The peasants and common people (who said they "could not see why the *first* royal baby should be called 'Ninety'") always spoke of her as the Princess Nobody. Only the Courtiers called her Niente. The Water Fairy was her godmother, but (for a Fairy reason) they concealed her *real* name, and of course, she was not *christened* Niente. Here you may see her sitting teaching the little Birds to sing. They are all round her in a circle, each of 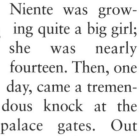 them singing his very best. Great fun she and all her little companions had with the Birds. And here you may see the baby Princess riding a Parrot, while one of her Maids of Honour teases an Owl. Never was there such a happy country; all Birds and Babies, playing together, singing, and as merry as the day was long.

This joyful life went on till the Princess

Niente was growing quite a big girl; she was nearly fourteen. Then, one day, came a tremendous knock at the palace gates. Out rushed the Porter, and saw a little Dwarf, wearing a red cap and a red cloak, riding a green Frog.

"Tell the King he is wanted," said the Dwarf.

The Porter carried this rude message, and the King went trembling to the door.

"I have come to claim your promise; you give me NIENTE," said the Dwarf, in his froggy voice.

Now the King had spoken long ago about his foolish promise, to the Queen of the Water Fairies, a very powerful person, and godmother of his child.

"The Dwarf must be one of *my* people, if he rides a Frog," the Queen of the Water Fairies had said. "Just send him to *me*, if he is troublesome." The King remembered this advice when he saw the Dwarf, so he put a bold face on it.

"That's you, is it?" said the King to the Dwarf. "Just you go to the Queen of the Water Fairies; she will have a word or two to say to you."

When the Dwarf heard that speech, it was *his* turn to tremble. He shook his little fist at the King; he half-drew his sword.

"I will have NIENTE yet," he scowled, and he set spurs to his Frog, and bounded off to pay a visit to the Queen of the Water Fairies.

It was night by the time the Dwarf reached the stream where the Queen lived, among the long flags and rushes and reeds of the river. Well, he and the Water Fairy had a long talk, and the end of it was that the Fairy found only one way of saving the Princess. She flew to the King and said, "I can only help you by making the Princess vanish clean away. I have a bird here on whose back she can fly away in safety. The Dwarf will not get her, but you will never see her again, unless a brave Prince can find her where she is hidden, and guarded by my Water Fairies."

Then the poor mother and father cried dreadfully, but they saw there was no hope. It was better that the Princess should vanish away, than that she should be married to a horrid rude Dwarf, who rode a Frog. So they sent for the Princess, and kissed her, and embraced her, and wept over her, and (gradually she faded out of their very arms, and vanished clean away) then she flew away on the bird's back.

2. IN MUSHROOM LAND

Now all of the kingdom next to Fairy Land was miserable, and all the people were murmuring, and the King and Queen were

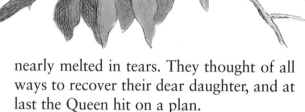

nearly melted in tears. They thought of all ways to recover their dear daughter, and at last the Queen hit on a plan.

"My dear," she said to the King, "let us offer to give our daughter for a wife, to any Prince who will only find her and bring her safely home."

"Who will want to marry a girl he can't see?" said the King. "If they have not married pretty girls they *can* see, they won't care for poor Niente."

"Never mind; we can only try," said the Queen. So she sent out messengers into all the world, and sent the picture of the Princess everywhere, and proclaimed that the beautiful Princess Niente, and no less than three-quarters of the kingdom would be given to the Prince who could find the Princess and bring her home. And there was to be a great tournament, or sham fight, at the palace, to amuse all the Princes before they went on the search. So many Princes gathered together, all full of hope; and they rode against each other with spears and swords, and knocked each other about, and afterwards dined and danced and made merry. Some Fairy Knights, too, came over the border, and they fought with

spears, riding Beetles and Grasshoppers, instead of horses. Here is a picture of a "joust", or tournament, between two sets of Fairy Knights. By all these warlike exercises, they increased their courage till they felt brave enough to fight all the Ghosts, and all the Giants, if only they could save the beautiful Princess.

Well, the tournaments were over, and off all the Princes went into Fairy Land. What funny sights they saw in Fairy Land! They saw a great snail race, the Snails running so fast that some of the Fairy jockeys fell off on the grass. They saw a Fairy dancing with a Squirrel, and they found all the birds, and all the beasts, quite friendly and kind, and able to talk like other people. This was the way in old times, but now no beasts talk, and no birds, except Parrots only.

Now among all the gallant army of Princes, one was ugly, and he looked old, and odd, and the rest laughed at him, and called him the Prince Comical. But he had a kind heart. One day, when he was out walking alone, and thinking what he could do to find the Princess, he saw three bad boys teasing a big Daddy Long Legs. They had got hold of one of his legs, and were

pulling at it with all their might. When the Prince Comical saw this, he ran up and drove the bad boys away, and rubbed the limb of the Daddy Long Legs, till he gave up groaning and crying. Then the Daddy Long Legs sat up, and said in a weak voice, "You have been very kind to me; what can I do for *you*?"

"Oh, help me," said the Prince, "to find the Princess Niente! *You* fly everywhere; don't you know where she is?"

"*I* don't know," said the Daddy Long Legs mournfully. "I have never flown so far. But I know that you are all in a very dangerous part of Fairy Land. And I will take you to an aged Black Beetle, who will be able to give you the best advice."

And with that, the Daddy Long Legs walked off with the Prince till they came to the Black Beetle.

"Can *you* tell this Prince," said the Daddy Long Legs, "where the Princess Niente is hidden?"

"I know it is in Mushroom Land," said the Beetle, "but he will want a guide."

"Will *you* be my guide?" asked the Prince.

"Yes," said the Beetle, "but what about your friends, the other Princes?"

"Oh, they must come too; it would not be fair to leave them behind," said the Prince Comical.

He was *the soul of honor*; and though the others laughed at him, he would not take advantage of his luck, and run away from them.

"Well, you *are* a true Knight," said the Black Beetle, "but before we go into the depths of Mushroom Land, just you come here with me."

Then the Black Beetle pointed out to the Prince a great smooth round red thing, a long way off.

"That is the first Mushroom in Mushroom Land," said the Beetle. "Now come with me, and you shall see what you shall see."

So the Prince followed the Beetle, till they came to the Mushroom.

"Climb up and look over," said the Beetle. So the Prince climbed up, and looked over. There he saw a King, who was wearing a crown, sound asleep.

Here is the Prince Comical (you see he is not very handsome!); and here is the King so sound asleep.

"Try to waken him," said the Beetle. "Just try."

So the Prince tried to waken the King, but it was of no use.

"Now, take warning by *that*," said the Black Beetle, "and never go to sleep under a Mushroom in Mushroom country. You will never wake, if you do, till the Princess Niente is found again."

Well, the Prince Comical said he would remember that, and he and the Beetle went off and found the other Princes. They were disposed to laugh at being led by a Black Beetle; but one of them, who was very learned, reminded them that armies had been led before by Woodpeckers, and Wolves, and Humming Birds.

So they all moved on, and at night they were very tired.

Now there were no houses, and not many trees, in Mushroom Land, and when night came all the Princes wanted to lie down under a very big Mushroom.

It was in vain that the Black Beetle and Prince Comical warned them to beware.

As they marched through Mushroom

Land the twilight came upon them, and the Elves began to come out for their dance, for Elves only dance at dusk, and they could not help joining them, which was very imprudent, as they had plenty to do the next day, and it would have been wiser if they had gone to sleep.

The Elves went on with their play till midnight, and exactly at midnight the Elves stopped their play, and undressed, and got up into the boughs of a big tree and went to sleep. You may wonder how the Elves know when it is midnight, as there are no clocks in Mushroom Land, of course. But they cannot really help knowing, as it is exactly at twelve that the Mushrooms begin to grow, and the little Mushrooms come up.

Now the Elves covered every branch of the tree, as you see in the picture, and the Princes did not know where to lie down. At last they decided to lie down under a very big Mushroom.

"Nonsense," they said. "*You* may sleep out in the open air, if you like; we mean to make ourselves comfortable here."

So they all lay down under the shelter of the Mushroom, and Prince Comical slept in the open air. In the morning he woke up, feeling very well and hungry, and off he set to call his friends. But he might as well have been calling the Mushroom itself. There they all lay under its shade; and though some of them had their eyes open, not one of them could move. The Prince shook them, dragged them, shouted at them, and pulled their hair. But the more he shouted and dragged, the louder they snored; and the worst of it was that he could not pull them out of the shadow of the Magic Mushroom. So there he had to leave them, sound asleep.

The Prince thought the Elves could help him perhaps, so he went and asked them how to waken his friends. They were all

awake, and the Fairies were dressing the baby-Elves. But they only said, "Oh! It's their fault for sleeping under a Mushroom. Anybody would know that is a very stupid thing to do. And besides, we have no time to attend to them, as the sun will be up soon, and we must get these Babies dressed and be off well before then."

"Why, where are you going to?" said the Prince.

"Ah! Nobody knows where we go to in the day time," said the Elves.

And nobody does.

"Well, what am I to do now?" said the Prince to the Black Beetle.

"*I* don't know where the Princess is," said the Beetle; "but the Blue Bird is very wise, and *he* may know. Now your best plan will be to steal two of the Blue Bird's eggs, and not give them back till he tells you all he can."

So off they set for the Blue Bird's nest; and, to make a long story short, the Prince stole two of the eggs, and would not give them back till the Bird promised to tell him all it knew. And the end of it was, that the Bird carried him to the court of the Queen of Mushroom Land. She was sitting on a Mushroom, wearing her crown, and she looked very funny and mischievous.

Here you see the Prince, with his hat off, kissing the Queen's hair, and asking for the Princess.

"Oh, *she's* quite safe," said the Queen of Mushroom Land, "but what a funny boy you are. You are not *half* handsome enough for the Princess Niente."

The poor Prince blushed. "They call me Prince Comical," said he. "I know I'm not half good enough!"

"You are *good* enough for anything," said the Queen of Mushroom Land, "but you might be prettier."

Then she touched him with her wand, and he became as handsome a Prince as ever was seen, wearing a beautiful red silk doublet, slashed with white, and a long gold-colored robe.

"*Now* you will do for my Princess Niente," said the Queen of Mushroom Land. "Blue Bird" (and she whispered in the Bird's ear), "take him away to the Princess Niente."

So they flew, and they flew, all day and all night, and the next day they came to a

green bower, all full of Fairies, and Butterflies, and funny little people. And there, with her long yellow hair round her, sat Princess Niente. And the Prince Charming laid his crown at her feet, and knelt on one knee, and asked the Princess to be his love and his lady. And she did not refuse him, so they were married in the church of the Elves, and the Glowworm sent his torches, and all the bells of all the flowers made a merry peal. And soon they were to travel home, to the King and Queen.

3. LOST AND FOUND

Now the Prince had found the Princess, and you might think that they had nothing to do but to go home again. The father and mother of the Princess were desperate to hear about her. Every day they climbed to the highest place in the castle, and looked across the plain, hoping to see dust on the road, and some brave Prince riding back with their daughter. But she never came, and their hair grew gray with sorrow and time. The parents of the other Princes, too, who were all asleep under the Mushroom, were alarmed about their sons, and feared they had been taken prisoners, or perhaps been eaten up by some Giant.

But Princess Niente and Prince Charming were lingering in the enchanted land, too happy to leave the flowers, the brooks, and the Fairies.

The faithful Black Beetle often whispered to the Prince that it was time to turn home-wards, but alas the Prince paid no more attention to his ally than if he had been an Ear-wig. So there, in the Valley Magical,

the Prince and Princess might be wandering to this day but for a very sad accident. The night they were married, the Princess had said to the Prince, "Now you may call me Niente, or any pet name you like; but never ever call me by my own name."

"But I don't know it," cried the Prince. "Do please tell me what it is?"

"Never," said the Princess; "you must never seek to know it."

"Why not?" said the Prince.

"Something dreadful will happen," said the Princess, "if ever you find out my name, and call me by it."

And she looked quite as if she could be very angry.

Now ever after this, the Prince kept wondering what his wife's real name could be, till he made himself quite unhappy.

"Is it Margaret?" he would say, when he thought the Princess was off her guard; or, "Is it Joan?" "Is it Dorothy?" "It can't be Sybil, can it?" But she would never tell him her name.

Now, one morning, the Princess awoke very early, but she felt so happy that she could not sleep. She lay awake and listened to the Birds singing, then watched a Fairy-boy teasing a Bird, which sang (so the boy said) out of tune, and another Fairy-baby riding on a Fly.

At last the Princess, who thought the Prince was sound asleep, began to croon softly a little song she had made about him and her. She had never told him about the song, partly because she was shy, and partly for another reason. So she crooned and hummed to herself,

Oh, hand in hand with Gwendoline,
While yet our locks are gold,
He'll fare among the forests green,
And through the gardens old;
And when, like leaves that lose
*   their green,*
Our gold has turned to gray,
Then, hand in hand with Gwendoline,
He'll fade and pass away!

"Oh, *Gwendoline* is your name, is it?" said the Prince, who had been wide awake, and listening to her song. And he began to laugh at having found out her secret, and tried to kiss her.

But the Princess turned very, very cold, and white like marble, so that the Prince began to shiver. He sat down on a fallen Mushroom, and hid his face in his hands, and, in a moment, all his beautiful hair vanished, and his splendid clothes, and his gold train, and his crown. He wore a red cap, and common clothes, and was Prince Comical once more. But the Princess arose, and she vanished swiftly away.

Here you see the poor Prince crying, and the Princess vanishing away. Thus he was punished for being curious and prying. It is natural, you will say, that a man should like to call his wife by her name. But the Fairies would not allow it, and, what is more, there are still some nations who will not allow a woman to mention the name of her husband.

Well, here was a sad state of things! The Princess was lost as much as ever, and Prince Charming was changed back into Prince Comical. The Black Beetle sighed day and night, and mingled his tears with those of the Prince. But neither of them knew what to do. They wandered about the Valley Magical, and though it was just as pretty as ever, it seemed quite ugly and stupid to them. The worst of it was that the Prince felt so foolish. After winning the greatest good fortune, and the dearest bride in the world, he had thrown everything away. He walked about crying, "Oh, Gwen—I mean oh, Niente! My dear Niente! Return to your own Prince Comical, and all will be forgiven!"

It is impossible to say what would have happened; and probably the Prince would have died of sorrow and hunger (for he ate nothing), if the Black Beetle had not one day met a Bat, which was the favorite charger of Puck. Now Puck, as all the world knows, is the Jester at the court of Fairy Land. He can make Oberon and

Titania—the King and Queen—laugh at the tricks he plays, and therefore they love him so much that there is nothing they would not do for him. So the Black Beetle began to talk about his master, the Prince, to the Bat Puck commonly rode; and the Bat, a most good-natured creature, told the whole story to Puck. Now Puck was also in a good humor, so he jumped at once on his Bat's back, and rode off to consult the King and Queen of Fairy Land. Well, they were sorry for the Prince—he had only broken one little Fairy law after all—and they sent Puck back to tell him what he was to do. This was to set off and find the Blue Bird again, and convince the Blue Bird to guide him to the home of the Water Fairy, the godmother of the Princess.

Long and far the Prince wandered, but at last he found the Blue Bird once more. And the Bird (so very good-naturedly) promised to fly in front of him till he led him to the beautiful stream, where the Water Fairy held her court. So they reached it at last, and then the Blue Bird harnessed himself to the chariot of the Water Fairy, and the chariot was the white cup of a water lily. Then he pulled, and pulled at the chariot (here he is dragging along the Water Fairy), till he brought her where the Prince was waiting. At first, when she saw him, she was rather angry. "Why did you find out my god-daughter's name?" she said; and the Prince had no excuse to make. He only turned red, and sighed. This rather pleased the Water Fairy.

very low bow, and thanked the Water Fairy. Then off he set, with the Blue Bird to guide him, in search of Mushroom Land. At long and at last he reached it, and glad he was to see the little sentinel on the border of the country.

All up and down Mushroom Land the Prince searched, and at last he saw his own Princess, and he rushed up, and knelt at her feet, and held out his hands to ask pardon for having disobeyed the Fairy law.

"Do you love the Princess very much?" said she.

"Oh, more than all the world," replied the Prince.

"Then back you go, to Mushroom Land, and you will find her in the old place. But perhaps she will not be pleased to forgive you at first."

The Prince thought he would chance *that,* but he did not say so. He only made a

But she was still rather cross, and down she jumped, and ran round the Mushroom, and he ran after her.

So he chased her for a minute or two, and at last she laughed, and popped up her head over the Mushroom, and pursed up her lips into a cherry. And he kissed her across the Mushroom, and he knew he had won back his own dear Princess; and, if it

were possible, they felt even happier than if they had never been parted.

"Journeys end in lovers meeting," and so do stories. The Prince has his Princess once again, and I can tell you they did not wait long, this time, in the Valley Magical. Off they went, straight home, and the Black Beetle guided them, flying in a bee-line. Just on the further border of Mushroom Land, they came to all the Princes fast asleep. But when the Princess drew near, they all wakened, and jumped up, and they slapped the fortunate Prince on the back, wished him luck, and cried out to him: "Hullo, Comical, old chap; we hardly knew you! Why, you've grown quite handsome!" And indeed he had; he was changed into Prince Charming again, but he was so happy that he never noticed it, for he was not conceited. But the Princess noticed it, and she loved him all the better. Then they all made a procession, with the Black Beetle marching at the head; in fact, they called him "Black Rod" now, and he was indeed quite a courtier.

So with flags flying, and music playing, they returned to the home of the Princess. And the King and Queen met them at the park gates, and fell on the neck of the Prince and Princess, and kissed them, and laughed, and cried for joy, and kissed them again. You may be sure the old Nurse was out among the foremost, her face quite shining with pleasure, and using longer words than the noblest there. And she admired the Prince very much, and was delighted that "her girl", as she called the Princess, had found such a good husband. So here we leave them, in that country which remained forever happy; that country which has neither history nor geography. So you won't find it on any map, nor can you read about it in any book but this one.

Here is a picture of the Prince and Princess at home, sitting on a beautiful rose, because a Fairy's god-child can do as she pleases.

As to the Black Beetle, he was appointed to a place about the court, but he never married, he had no children, and consequently there are no *other* Black Beetles in the country where the Prince and Princess became King and Queen.

Queen of the Pirate Isle

Adapted by Alice Mills

A long time ago there lived a girl called Polly. She lived in a time when girls wore sashes around their waists and petticoats underneath their dresses. Her brother's name was Hickory, and he wore knickerbockers. They lived in California during the time of the gold rush, when men from all over the world came to seek their fortune by digging for gold, and Chinese people set up market gardens to feed all these hungry workers. Polly and Hickory's best friend was a Chinese boy, called Wan Lee, and he used to wear a blue shirt and wide blue trousers, with his hair tied back in a pigtail.

Polly's mother and father lived an ordinary life in an ordinary house, but Polly lived an extraordinary life. Her family was never sure from day to day which Polly would come out of her bedroom to join them for breakfast. Some mornings she woke up and decided that it was a good day to be a beggar child. Then she put on a beautifully tattered old shawl that her mother had thrown away and Polly had rescued. When she wrapped it tightly round her shoulders and shivered, she looked like a sad little beggar girl shivering with the cold.

Sometimes she was Polly the schoolteacher, and then she used to sit on a stool and wave a stick in the air, looking very strict. When she was Polly the teacher, she always suspected that her students had not done their homework or read their books, but the truth was that she had not read the little brown book, and if anyone had dared to question her about it, she would not know the answers either. But she relied on looking fierce and waving her big stick and said that it was her job to ask the questions and her students' job to answer, not the other way around.

Sometimes, when Polly woke up, it was a good day to be a very proud lady. She held her nose in the air, looking down at everyone and everything. Unfortunately, this meant that she always made a mess when she was eating, because she could not see what was on her plate. It was much easier to be a proud lady when she was standing up, with a huge sash across one shoulder and an enormous spear. The spear was only for show, because, being such a proud person, she would not dream of such a common and ordinary thing as getting into a fight.

Polly the proud lady kept her nose high in the air when she walked. Her spear was too long and awkward to take with her when she was walking, so she used to carry her umbrella instead and wear a splendid ostrich feather. The proud lady strutted when she walked, lifting each foot high into the air, so that she could only take very slow steps and always came home last. But because she was so proud and so much better than anyone else, she just looked down her nose at them for walking like ordinary people. And sometimes she tried walking with her eyes shut, as she was too proud to look at ordinary everyday things, and then she used to bump into everything and her walks became very short indeed.

Polly especially liked being the Queen of the Pirate Isle with Hickory and Wan Lee as her subjects. Her reign began one day when she was a pirate, traveling around the world with Wan Lee and Hickory in a little boat. She had a chair to sit on next to the mast, so that she could hold onto it and not get swept overboard if the seas became rough, but on this day, a terrible storm began to rage, so strongly that Polly lost her grip on the mainmast and along with Hickory and Wan Lee, she was washed overboard.

The boat capsized and they had to swim for their lives. Luckily the sea was quite warm and they did not attract any sharks, but after several hours of swimming, Polly became very tired. Hickory noticed that she could hardly move her arms and legs through the waves, and he turned back and swam over to her, lifting her onto his back. Then he swam forwards again, telling her that he had seen a glimpse of a desert island far away, right on the horizon. Hickory's arms and legs were now getting weary, but he bravely kept swimming for miles and miles through the tropical sea until they reached the island.

When they reached the land, Wan Lee searched for food to keep them from starving. All he could find was a packet of peppermints, just enough to keep them alive until lunchtime. Now that they were all alone on their desert island, they made it into their kingdom. A kingdom needs a king or queen to rule it, and they all agreed to make Polly the queen of the island, ruling over Hickory and Wan Lee, the fiercest pirates who had ever lived. She was a very strict queen, always sending her subjects to bed at the end of an adventure. They survived many storms at sea and found chests full of treasure, and there was always plenty to tell the nursemaid at teatime.

One day Wan Lee and Hickory quarrelled over who was the

bravest of all pirates. Hickory boasted about all the treasures he had found, all the battles he had won and all the storms he had sailed through, but Wan Lee said, "You would not be nearly so brave on land. I dare you to do pirate deeds in the country where Queen Polly's parents live, and that will show if you are really a pirate or not." Hickory got very red in the face and shouted, "I will go there tomorrow and come back with buckets full of treasure, just you see," and Queen Polly thought that she had better come along with them too.

The house where Polly lived was not far from a canyon where men were looking for gold. Polly, Wan Lee and Hickory liked to sit in the canyon and watch, sitting on a fallen pine tree and listening to the men calling to each other. Now and then a waggon passed by, carrying men and mining tools but never much gold. Polly

had not been to visit the canyon since she became Queen of the Pirate Isle, and so none of the miners knew that the fine lady sitting in splendor on the tree trunk was really visiting royalty.

Wan Lee met Hickory and Polly at the fallen pine tree, and with him came his friend Pat in search of an adventure. Pat's idea of an adventure was to go hunting for bears, but he soon joined in the three pirates' test of bravery. He told them that real pirates never wore shoes. Instead, they coated their feet with mud to harden the skin so that they could climb the rigging of their ship barefoot. Hickory, Polly and Wan Lee followed Pat to a muddy pool where they all took off their shoes and covered their feet with mud.

Then they sat in the sun until the mud dried, and after that they were ready to go on an adventure. But the dry mud kept falling off their feet, and they decided that they would wear their shoes—all except Pat, who liked the feel of the grass under his feet. They went looking for treasure together, and first they looked in the grass, just in case the miners had dropped any rocks gleaming with gold, but they could see nothing that looked at all like gold lying on the ground, only those endless blades of grass.

On the side of the canyon were the mouths of the tunnels where the miners were working, looking for a vein of gold in the dark rocks. "I'd like to go into one of those tunnels," Polly said to herself, and suddenly all the pirates had the same idea. They would go into one of the tunnels and surprise the men working inside, and demand their surrender. Then they would capture the mine and hoist the pirate flag and seize all the gold.

send the heavy tools down the hill like this than to carry them uphill, but the track was so steep and slippery that no-one had ever climbed down it. Now the bold pirates started to walk down, but suddenly Pat slipped and started sliding down the track, and after him came Hickory tumbling down, then Polly and her doll, and lastly Wan Lee. Down and down they slid, until they reached a place where a little tree was growing by the side of the track. Pat grabbed hold of the branches and stopped himself sliding any further, and then down tumbled Polly after him, then Hickory and Wan Lee. It was good to hold onto the branches

The pirates made a bold and daring plan. They would creep up the side of the hill so that they could take the miners by surprise from above their diggings. The men always climbed up into the tunnels from the valley below, and they would never expect enemies to burst into their mine from above. It was a long climb and first they went on tip-toe, then they walked, then they scrambled, and for the last part they climbed on their hands and knees.

Down the hill went a steep track that the miners used to slide equipment down to the top tunnel. It was easier for them to

for a moment and catch their breath. Then they noticed a dark opening in the hillside, not far from the track. It was not a tunnel made by men, but a cave.

"Look," said Wan Lee. "The rocks are all glittering with treasure!" The walls of the cave

shone where the sunlight could reach them, but it was a silvery brightness, not like the gold that they were hoping for.

Into the cave they went, walking as quietly as they could just in case other pirates had found the cave first, and were lying in wait for them. It was very dark inside the cave and the ground was hard and stony underneath their feet. Pat was sorry that he had left his shoes behind and

said that he could not go any further.

So out they came again and sat down in the sunlight, to make a pirate plan. They needed something to light their way into the cave, but for that they would have to go home again or else ask the miners, and the children wanted to keep the

shining treasure-cave their secret. Hickory and Wan Lee started to argue again, and Queen Polly was just about to tell them to be quiet, because the miners would hear them, when she noticed something dreadful had happened to her doll. "Lady Mary's hair has gone!" she said. "She must have lost it when we tumbled down the hill, or maybe in the cave. We must go back and look for it."

But everyone was so tired, after their long walk and then their slide and tumble, and then their visit to the cave.

They just wanted to sit for a minute or two, before searching for the doll's lost hair, and then they felt like closing their eyes. Soon they were all asleep, with the shorn doll lying across Queen Polly's lap.

Polly was the first to wake up. She was ready for an adventure again, and she was just going to wake up the others when she noticed her doll, lying on a rock. How pale Lady Mary looked, in her white dress with a bare scalp. Perhaps she had caught a cold in the chilly cave and was shivering, even though the sun was shining warm and bright.

Polly sat down again and hugged Lady Mary close, to keep her warm. She remembered when she had been a beggar girl, with her parents buried in the churchyard, and how she had wrapped herself in a big black mourning cloak made out of an old curtain, and sat sadly among the tombstones. Perhaps she would go into mourning for poor Lady Mary next, and sit sadly in the churchyard again, in her mourning cloak. Polly's eyelids drooped again, and very soon she was fast asleep.

When she woke up, she was being carried gently down the hill by one of the miners, his face and arms all black and red from the earth that he had been digging in. He asked "Is there any command Your Majesty would like to give us?" and Polly smiled a very big smile, because he had called her "your majesty". "No, thank you," she said, and then the miner asked, "Is there anything Your Majesty has lost?" In his hand was Lady Mary's missing hair.

Queen Polly could see Hickory and Wan Lee and Pat, all being carried down the hill, fast asleep. When they came to the mine tunnels, the miners woke them up and asked if they would like

158

to see inside one of the mines, as a reward. "A reward for what?" asked Wan Lee. "For finding the lode of gold in the cave," said the miner. The cave that the children had discovered was the place the miners had been searching so long for, where the gold ran in a thick vein through the rocks, deep into the hillside. Now they all declared a holiday from work, to celebrate the finding of the lode. Inside the tunnel, the miners all made themselves into pirates, in honour of Queen Polly and her pirate band.

Then the big bearded pirates lifted the Queen and her pirate crew into one of their waggons, and they began to glide back through the tunnel and out into the warm sunshine. Lady Mary was still feeling cold, but looked a little better now that she knew her hair had been found. It was time to go home and sew her well again. One of the miners had a needle and thread and sewed Lady Mary's hair back again (he was not very good at it and the poor doll's hair fell off soon afterwards) and then the miners said that they would carry the pirates home in honor of their great discovery.

Down to the bottom of the canyon they went, and the miners all made a guard of honour for the waggon as it rolled past. Then they lifted the children out again and started carrying them along until they came to Polly's house. Polly's mother was startled at the sight of the big bearded miners carrying in the four children, all wide awake now and eager to tell her about their adventure. But one of the miners was the first to say anything. "Here is your daughter," he said to Polly's mother, "home again safe and sound."

"What have the children been playing at?" asked Polly's mother, and the miner told her about the track that they had slipped and slid down, and the sparkling cave they had found, and the vein of gold that the miners had discovered there.

Then he went down on one knee before Polly and said to her, "So now we are all loyal subjects of her Royal Majesty Polly, the Queen of the Pirate Isle."

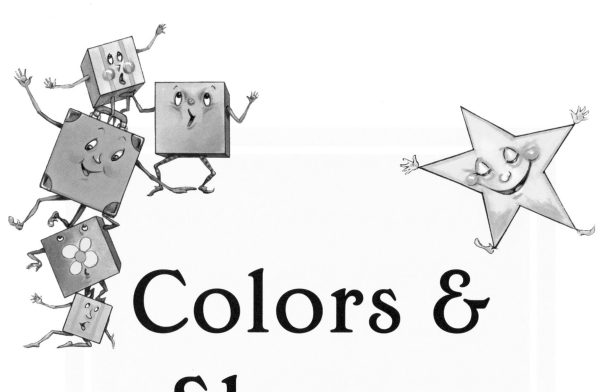

Colors & Shapes

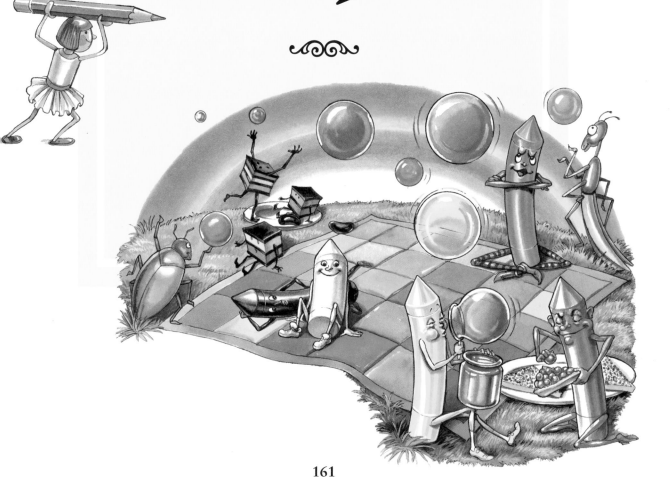

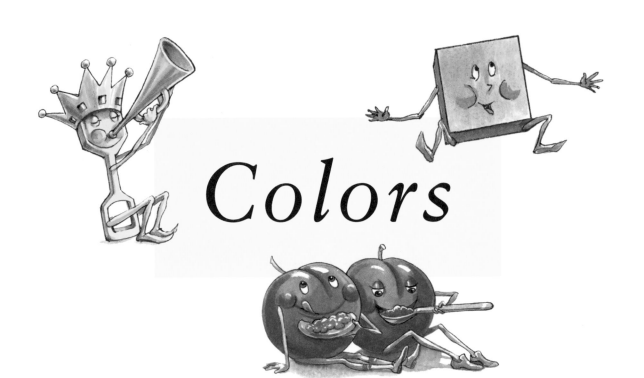

Colors

red

There are many different kinds of red.

What red things can you find in the picture?

blue

There are many different kinds of blue.

What blue things can you find in the picture?

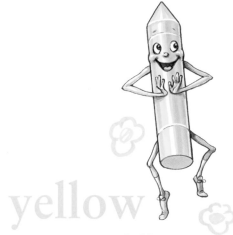

yellow

There are many different kinds of yellow.

What yellow things can you find in the picture?

red + blue =

purple

If you mix red
and blue together
you make purple.

yellow + red =

orange

If you mix yellow
and red together
you make orange.

yellow **+** blue **=**

green

If you mix yellow
and blue together
you make green.

yellow **+** red **+** blue **=**

brown

If you mix yellow

and red and blue together
you make brown.

white

What white things can you
find in the picture?

red + white =

pink

If you mix red
and white together
you make pink.

black

What **black** things can you
find in the picture?

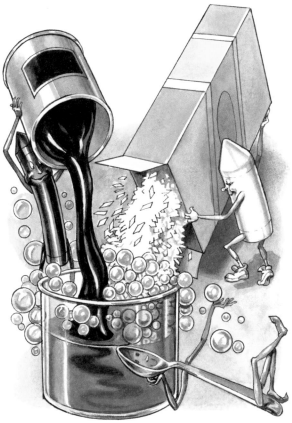

black + white =

gray

If you mix **black**
and white together
you make gray.

Can you name
all the different colors
in this picture?

Shapes

Circle

The plates and saucers race and clatter
And roll in circles while the platter
Calls out, "Take care! Don't fall and shatter!"

How many circles can you find in the picture?
Look on page 176 for some clues.

Square

They're practicing their circus trick,
Some like it high and some feel sick.
One near the top needs helping, quick!

How many squares can you find in the picture?
Look on page 176 for some clues.

Triangle

Triangle cheese and triangle snack,
Some mice are lurking at the back,
Ready to launch a snack attack!

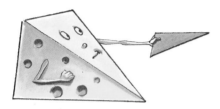

How many triangles can you find in the picture?
Look on page 176 for some clues.

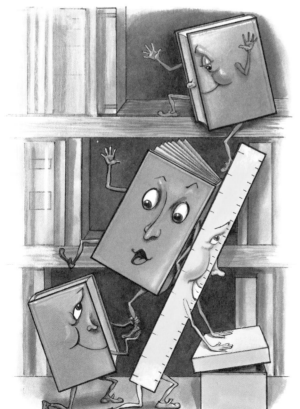

Rectangle

The books decided to slide out.
"Rectangles rule!" I heard them shout.
I did not leave them lying about!

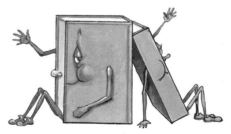

How many rectangles can you find in the picture?
Look on page 176 for some clues.

Oval

Five oval eggs lie in the nest.
Don't touch, don't steal, don't be a pest!
Seeing the babies hatch is best.

How many ovals can you find in the picture?
Look on page 177 for some clues.

Crescent

The curved moon says with friendly glance,
"Come to my party,
take a chance,
Just smile a crescent
smile and dance!"

How many crescents can you find in the picture?
Look on page 177 for some clues.

Diamond

The diamond puppet leaps and springs,
The kites fly high on diamond wings,
I long to fly—where are my strings?

How many diamonds can you find in the picture?
Look on page 177 for some clues.

Heart

Where have the heart-shaped chocolates gone?
Out of their box I watched them run.
I did not eat a single one!

How many hearts can you find in the picture?
Look on page 177 for some clues.

Star

I ran to catch a falling star,
I looked in rockpools near and far
And found it where the starfish are.

How many stars can you find in the picture?
Look on page 178 for some clues.

Cone

If only cones could party too!
If only magic could come true!
The pencil's power is there for you
To play with shapes and make things new!

How many cones can you find in the picture?
Look on page 178 for some clues.

Can you name
all the different shapes
in this picture?

Answers

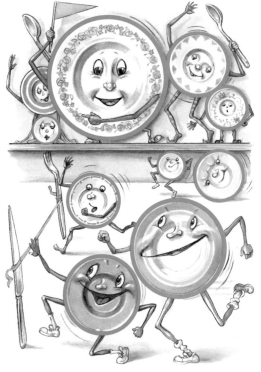

Did you find these circles
in the picture on page 170?

Did you find these squares
in the picture on page 170?

Did you find these triangles
in the picture on page 171?

Did you find these rectangles
in the picture on page 171?

Answers

Did you find these ovals
in the picture on page 172?

Did you find these crescents
in the picture on page 172?

Did you find these diamonds
in the picture on page 173?

Did you find these hearts
in the picture on page 173?

Answers

Did you find these stars
in the picture on page 174?

Did you find these cones
in the picture on page 174?

Alphabets
& Numbers

ABC of *Funny Animals*

Ass,
adder,
ape

Bear,
badger,
boa

Crocodile,
camel

Dog,
duck,
duckling

Elephant,
eel

Fox,
fish,
frog

Giraffe, gorilla

Hyena, hippopotamus

Ibis, ibex

Jackal

Kangaroo, kiwi

I J K

Lion,
leopard

Magpie,
mouse,
monkey

Newt

Owl,
opossum

P

Pig,
porcupine,
pelican

Quagga,
quasje

Q

Rhinoceros,
ram,
rabbit

Stork,
swan,
squirrel

Tortoise,
turkey

Urson (Canadian
porcupine)

Vampire bat,
vulture

Wolf,
walrus,
wish-ton-wish
(Prairie dog)

Xihias
(Swordfish)

Yak,
Yamma
(Llama)

Zebra

a b c
d e f g h
i j k l
m n o p
q r s t u
v w x
y z.

Twenty-Six Nonsense Rhymes and Pictures

The **A**bsolutely **A**bstemious **A**ss,
who resided in a barrel,
and only lived on soda water and
pickled cucumbers.

The **B**ountiful **B**eetle,
who always carried a green
umbrella when
it didn't rain,
and left it at home when
it did.

The **C**omfortable **C**onfidential **C**ow,
who sat in her red Morocco
armchair
and toasted her own
bread in the
parlor fire.

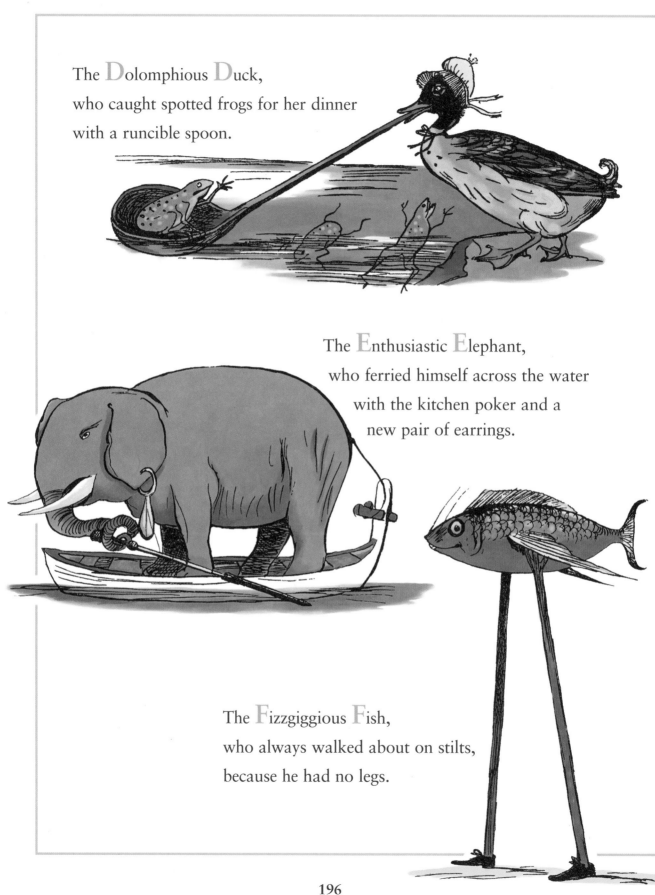

The Dolomphious Duck,
who caught spotted frogs for her dinner
with a runcible spoon.

The Enthusiastic Elephant,
who ferried himself across the water
with the kitchen poker and a
new pair of earrings.

The Fizzgiggious Fish,
who always walked about on stilts,
because he had no legs.

The Goodnatured Gray Gull,
who carried the old owl, and his
   crimson carpet-bag,
across the river, because he
   could not swim.

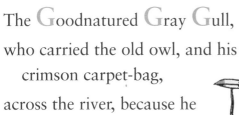

The Hasty Higgledy-piggledy
   Hen,

who went to market in a blue
   bonnet and shawl,
and bought a fish for her supper.

The Inventive Iguana,
who caught a remarkable rabbit in a
stupendous silver spoon.

The Judicious Jubilant Jay,
who did up her back hair every
    morning
with a wreath of roses, three
    feathers, and a gold pin.

The Kicking Kangaroo,
who wore a pale pink muslin dress
    with blue spots.

The Lively Learned Lobster,
who mended his own clothes
with a needle and thread.

The Melodious Meritorious Mouse,
who played a merry minuet
  on the pianoforte.

The Nutritious Newt,
who purchased a round plum pudding
  for his grand-daughter.

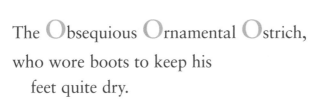

The Obsequious Ornamental Ostrich,
who wore boots to keep his
  feet quite dry.

The Perpendicular Purple Polly,
who read the newspaper with his
spectacles and ate parsnip pie.

The Queer Querulous Quail,
who smoked a pipe of tobacco
on the top of a tin tea kettle.

The Rural Runcible
Raven,
who wore a white wig and
flew away
with a carpet broom.

The Scroobious Snake,
who always wore a hat on his head,
for fear he should bite anybody.

The Tumultuous
Tom-tommy Tortoise,
who beat a drum all day long
in the middle of the
wilderness.

The Umbrageous Umbrella-maker,
whose face nobody ever saw
because it was always covered by his
umbrella.

The 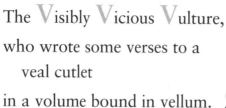Visibly Vicious Vulture,
who wrote some verses to a
    veal cutlet
in a volume bound in vellum.

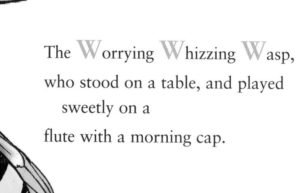

The Worrying Whizzing Wasp,
who stood on a table, and played
    sweetly on a
flute with a morning cap.

The Excellent Double-extra XX,
imbibing King Xerxes,
who lived a long while ago.

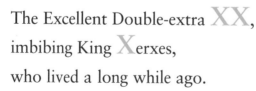

The Yonghy-Bonghy-Bo,
whose head was ever so much
    bigger than his body,
and whose hat was rather small.

The Zigzag Zealous Zebra,
who carried five monkeys on his back
all the way to Jellibolee.

A Apple Pie

A
apple pie

B en
bit it

C aitlin
cut it

Donna
dealt it

Ebony
ate it

Felix
fought for it

Gus
got it

Harry
had it

Isis sat idle while

Jeremy jumped for it

Kiah
knelt for it

Lola
longed for it

Mohammed
mourned
for it

Noah
nodded for it

Olivia
opened it

Pandora
peeped in it

Quincy
quartered it

Rhiannon
ran for it

Shani
sang for it

Tilly took it

Umina, Vashti, Willow,
Xaviera, Yoorana, Zoe
all had a large
slice and went
off to bed.

Tin Tan Numbers

The Tin Tans are funny folk,
They eat and sing and dance and talk;
They live in kitchens and in rooms,
Are made of saucers, cups and spoons;
Of teapots, forks, tomato cans,
Of clocks, pie-rollers, pots and pans.
Their clothes are made of brass and tin,
Some are quite stout, some rather thin;
But all have legs and arms and hands,
And can be found in all the lands.
BUT
As soon as you enter the kitchen
and rooms,
They dissolve into common saucers
and spoons.

1 **One** bad-tempered kettle
Began to boil and bellow,
Bubbling till he blew his top off,
What an angry fellow!

2 Two old-fashioned irons,
Love to stop and chatter,
What they hate is working hard—
Does laundry really matter?

3 Three clocks play at circus time,
Juggling and catching balls,
Keeping their balance on the rope—
I do hope no-one falls!

4

The jug is leaking water,
Plip plop! Plip plop! Plip plop!
Four Tin Tans try to wake him up
And catch each falling drop.

5

Five Tin Tans go out walking
They're all lined up to start.
With hat and fan and walking boots,
With stockings striped and smart.

6 Six fine Tin Tans take their partners,
Dancing high or kneeling low.
Move together to the music,
Lift a knee and point a toe.

7 Six Tin Tans playing hide and seek,
Are tiptoeing and leaping,
If only they would turn their heads,
They'd spot number **seven** peeping.

8 Eight sad Tin Tans sulking,
Feeling very low,
Crabby, tired and grumpy,
Full of gloom and woe.

9 We need more players for our team,
There's only eight of us.
Be number **nine**, join in the fun,
Say yes! Don't make a fuss!

10

Ten

Making ice-cream in a churn,
Mix it, blend it, beat it.
Tin Tans say they're hungry now,
They only want to eat it!

11

Eleven

Tin Tans want some ice-cream,
Pile it very high, make haste!
Slipping, falling, snatching, stealing,
Too much haste makes lots of waste.

12 With hats, flags and waving arms,
Twelve Tin Tans say goodbye.
Already one has fallen in,
Let's hope the rest keep dry.

13 Here come **thirteen** Tin Tans,
Over the springboard they dash,
tumbling into the water,
What a mighty splash!

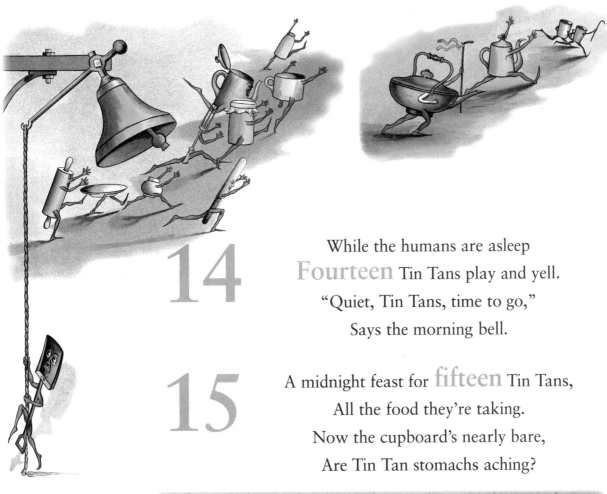

14 While the humans are asleep
Fourteen Tin Tans play and yell.
"Quiet, Tin Tans, time to go,"
Says the morning bell.

15 A midnight feast for fifteen Tin Tans,
All the food they're taking.
Now the cupboard's nearly bare,
Are Tin Tan stomachs aching?

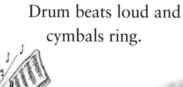

16

Sixteen Tin Tans making music,
Some can dance and some can sing.
Sweetly sound the flute and fiddle,
Drum beats loud and
cymbals ring.

17 As the cloth falls from the table,
Seventeen Tin Tans slip and slide.
Did it fall? Did someone pull it?
Naughty teaspoons run and hide.

18

19

Seventeen Tin Tans watching tennis
Plus the player, that's eighteen.

On this side there's eighteen cheering,
Add the player to make nineteen.

20 **Twenty** Tin Tans on parade,
Running, marching, hopping;
Waving arms and waving flags,
They're never ever stopping!

Nursery Rhymes

Old Mother Hubbard

Old Mother Hubbard went to
    the cupboard,
To get her poor dog a bone;
But when she came there the
    cupboard was bare,
And so the poor dog had none.

She went to the baker's
To buy him some bread,
But when she came back
The poor dog was dead.

She went to the joiner's
To buy him a coffin,
But when she came back
The poor dog was laughing.

She went to the hatter's
To buy him a hat,
But when she came back
He was feeding the cat.

She went to the tavern
For white wine and red,
But when she came back
The dog stood on his head.

She took a clean dish
To get him some tripe,
But when she came back
He was smoking a pipe.

She went to the fruiterer's
To buy him some fruit,
But when she came back
He was playing the flute.

She went to the barber's
To buy him a wig,
But when she came back
He was dancing a jig.

She went to the cobbler's
To buy him some shoes,
But when she came back
He was reading the news.

She went to the hosier's
To buy him some hose,
But when she came back
He was dressed in his
    clothes.

She went to the tailor's
To buy him a coat,
But when she came back
He was riding a goat.

The dame made a curtsy,
The dog made a bow;
The dame said, "Your servant,"
The dog said, "Bow wow."

The Story of Rich Mrs Duck

When Mrs Duck waddled out, she kept wheezing and puffing,
Which her friends said arose from over-eating and stuffing;
She observed other ducks, as she passed along, stop,
And make vulgar remarks on the size of her crop;
She added every day something rich to her dinner,
But to her friends she declared she got thinner and thinner.

One day from the gutter she'd returned scarce a minute,
After finding and gobbling many rich morsels in it,
When she felt very queer—her head swimming round,
Until she came near falling flat on the ground.
She tried this and that, but was forced in the end,
As she kept getting worse, for a doctor to send.

Dr Drake kept a shop of
    dimensions not large,
In a hole in the dung-hill
    by the side of the yard,
Where he dispensed certain
    stones, and one or two
    gravels,
With sundry rare herbs he
    had found in his travels.
And this Dr Drake, by
    very good luck,
Was called in to prescribe
    for rich Mrs Duck:
So brushing his clothes,
    and putting his feathers
    in order,
He waddled off to attend
    to the lady's disorder.

On entering her house, he found his patient extended
Quite back in her chair, with her crop much distended.
"Dr Drake," she exclaimed, "I feel greatly depressed,
Dizzy sight, very faint, and a load at my chest.
You must know, my dear sir, that I never exceed
What is wholesome and proper in drink and in feed,
And to one who's so dainty, it certainly is hard
To suffer such sharp, racking pain in the gizzard;
I strongly suspect it proceeds from the cramp,
For I remember being out the other day in the damp."

The Doctor looked wise—then shook his learned head,
And feeling her cold flabby paw, he thus said,
"Permit me, dear Madam, your tongue now to see;"
Then, timing her pulse, "I'm thinking," said he,
"Your disorder arises from over-eating and drinking,
And your pulse is so low, without care you'll be sinking!"

Quoth the lady, incensed at
    so rude a remark,
"I'm sure, Dr Drake, you
    are quite in the dark;
From aught that I
    eat it can't
    possibly be,
For I'm careful,
    indeed, to an
    extraordinary
    degree."

But the Doctor, at once, without more ado,
Commenced bleeding and blistering, with an emetic or two;
And just as he thought that his patient looked better,
She gave a roll of the eyes, and a terrible flutter,
Fell first on her back, and then on her side,
Gave an awful loud
     quack—a struggle
     —and died!

Her friends all assembled near
    a neighboring swamp,
And buried the rich lady with
    much funeral pomp;
This inscription, I'm told, her
    tombstone they put on,
"Here lies Mrs Duck, the nasty
    old glutton;"
And old Ducks their young
    Ducklings oft bring here to
    teach
The sad shameful end that a
    glutton may reach.

Old Dame Trot, and her Comical Cat

Old Dame Trot set off to the fair,

With her cat on her shoulder, to
see the folks there;

The people all laughed as they
saw them go by,

Says the Dame, "I'll laugh, too,"
but says Pussy, "I'll cry."

She went to the
dairy, to buy her
some milk;

When she came
back, Puss was
sewing some silk.

She went to the fish
shop, and bought
her some fish;

When she came
back, Puss was
washing a dish.

She went to the
miller's, to grind
her some corn;

When she came
back, Puss was
blowing a horn.

She went to the
fruit shop, to buy
her a plum;

When she came
back, Puss was
beating a drum.

She went to the
glover's, for
gloves very small,

While Puss at
croquet was hit-
ting a ball.

She went to the
florist's, to buy
her a rose;

When she came
back, Pussy
stood on
her nose.

She went off the next time, and bought her a hat;

When she came back, Puss was catching a rat.

Then off to the baker's, but back again quick,

For Puss at Aunt Sally was throwing a stick.

She bought her some boots
of a very bright red;

But when she came back,
she found Pussy in bed.

She went to the cloak shop,
and bought her a cloak;

When she came back again,
Puss had not awoke.

She went into town,
to buy crinoline,

While Pussy was
trying to wash
herself clean.

She went to the
furrier's, and bought
her some fur;

Says the Dame, "Do
you like it?" and
Pussy said, "Purr!"

She bought her a dress
of a lovely sky-blue;

Says Dame Trot, "Say,
thank you;" but
Pussy said, "Mew."

We Love our Cat

Who's up to mischief? It's not us,
It must be puss.

Who tore my slipper so it's shabby?
Must be tabby.

Who hid my bag, my boot and mitten?
Blame the kitten.

Who teased and terrified the doggie?
Must be moggie.

Who left stuff lying anyhow?
Meow! Meow!

He's naughty but, despite all that
We love our cat.

I Can be Anything

I can be a monster,
I can be a queen,
I can be a ladybird
Or something in between.

I can be a dinosaur,
I can be a snail,
Practicing my mighty roar,
Silvering a trail.

Don't be fooled by outsides,
That's not all we are,
I can be a porcupine,
A candle shining far,
Inside me is everything
From speck of dust to star.

Umbrellas

Whenever we go for a walk,
We always take umbrellas;
We recommend this trusty friend
For town or country dwellers.

If skies grow dark and clouds grow thick
And rain comes falling steady,
We're good as gold, we have been told,
Umbrellas at the ready.

But if the sky is perfect blue
And out you go as we did,
You'll hear folks say, "No rain today!
Umbrellas are not needed."

But when the sun grows burning hot,
And folks are seeking shelter,
Umbrellas give the shade you need
While others sweat and swelter.

Picking Flowers

I'm picking flowers in the grass,
Dandelion, daisy.
A daisy is the day's bright eye,
Watching the sun as he goes by,
Except when skies are hazy.

I'm picking flowers in the grass,
Daisy, dandelion.
A dandelion wears each petal
Like flashing sword of burning
    metal
Or teeth of golden lion.

At the Table

My chair is much too tall for me
When we sit at the table;
If mother did not help me up
I just would not be able
To join her at the table.

To gain some height I could wear heels,
I've thought of wearing flippers,
I want to use the little step
Where grown-ups rest their slippers,
Much easier than flippers.

I'd climb the step and reach my seat,
I'd do it so politely,
Then down I'd jump without a thump,
I'd land so very lightly,
I'd do it most politely.

We have to climb them sideways,
Like ladders.

Sleepy Harry

Sleepyhead, sleepyhead,
Sun down, it's time for bed.

Nightfall and evening star,
Dreams carry you afar.

Clear skies, wind or rain,
Bring you safely home again.

Moonlight, watch over you,
Sleeping softly all night through.

Baby's Laughing Eyes

Everything is new for babies,
Shape and sound and size,
Touching, tasting, fearless,
Each moment a surprise.

Far too much we take for granted,
Habit dulls our eyes.
Babies help us to remember
Where true wonder lies.

I love to see my world afresh
Through baby's laughing eyes.

I Wish Today
were Yesterday

I do not care, I did not care,
I will not care tomorrow
I only want to laugh and play—
Now hear my tale of sorrow.

I would not wash or brush my hair,
Now it's all grease and tangle;
My clothes I wore until they tore,
And now they're hang-a-dangle.

I did not care, I would not care
For breakfast, lunch or dinner,
Instead I stuffed myself with snacks,
I wish that I were thinner.

A year ago of yesterdays
I lived quite free of sorrow,
I wish today were yesterday
And yesterday tomorrow.

Susan Blue

Oh, Susan Blue,
How do you do?
Please may I go for a
  walk with you?
Where shall we go:
Oh, I know—
Down in the meadow
  where the
  cowslips grow!

Wishes

Oh, if you were a little boy,
And I was a little girl—
Why you would have some whiskers grow
And then my hair would curl.

Ah! If I could have whiskers grow,
I'd let you have my curls;
But what's the use of wishing it—
Boys never can be girls.

Miss Molly and the Little Fishes

Oh, sweet Miss Molly,
You're so fond
Of fishes in a little pond.
And perhaps they're glad
To see you stare
With such bright eyes
Upon them there.
And when your fingers and your
  thumbs
Drop slowly in the small white
  crumbs,
I hope they're happy. Only this—
When you've looked long enough,
  sweet miss.
Then, most beneficent young giver,
Restore them to their native river.

To Mystery Land

Oh, dear, how will it end?
Peggy and Susie how naughty you are.
You little know where you are,
Going so far, and so high,
Nearly up to the sky.
Perhaps it's a giant who lives there,
And perhaps it's a lovely princess.
But you very well know
You've no business to go;
You'll get yourselves into a mess.

Oh, dear, I'm sure it is true;
Whatever on earth can it matter to you?
For you know it—oh, fie—
That it's naughty to pry
Into other's affairs—
Into other folks houses to go,
Where you know
You're not asked.
So you'd better come
While there's time, it is plain.
Go home—and be never
So naughty again.

On the Wall Top

Dancing and prancing to town we go,
On the top of the wall of the town we go.
Shall we talk to the stars, or
talk to the moon,
Or run along home to our
dinner so soon?

239

The Tea Party

In the pleasant green garden
We sat down to tea;
"Do you take sugar?" and
"Do you take milk?"
She'd got a new gown on—
A smart one of silk.
We all were as happy
As happy could be,
On that bright summer's day
When she asked us to tea.

On the Bridge

If I could see a little fish—
That is what I just now wish!
I want to see his great round eyes
Always open in surprise.

I wish a water-rat would glide
Slowly to the other side;
Or a dancing spider sit
On the yellow flags a bit.

I think I'll get some stones to throw,
And watch the pretty circles show.
Or shall we sail a flower-boat,
And watch it slowly—slowly float?

That's nice—because you never
    know
How far away it means to go;
And when tomorrow comes,
    you see,
It may be in the great wide sea.

Ball

One—two, is one to you;
One—two—three, is one to me.
Throw it fast
    or not at all,
And mind you do
    not let it fall.

Cross Patch

Cross Patch, lift the latch,
Sit by the fire and spin;
Take a cup, and drink it up,
Then call your neighbors in.

To London

One foot up, the other
　foot down,
That's the way to
　London-town.

Bonny Johnny

Johnny shall have a new bonnet,
And Johnny shall go to the fair;
And Johnny shall have a blue ribbon,
To tie up his bonny brown hair.

Little Tommy Tittlemouse

Little Tommy Tittlemouse,
Lived in a little house;
He caught fishes
In other men's ditches.

Dash's Holiday

Said Dash, a young and handsome dog,
"While mistress is away,
I'll run out to the fresh green fields,
And take a holiday.

"My cousin keeps a farmer's flocks;
And pleased I'm sure he'll be,
A grand relation like myself
At his poor house to see."

So Dash drew on his Sunday coat
Of velvet, soft and red;
And a fine hat, with snow-white plume,
He put upon his head.

And thus he walked through many
   streets
—A puppy young and vain—
And pitied all the "vulgar" folks
Who must in town remain.

For many miles he walked and ran,
And seldom paused to rest;
Until he met a snow-white dog
Like a rural lassie dressed.

She wore a hat and bodice
   blue;
A wheatsheaf on her arm;
Dash bowed, and said,
   "Please tell me, ma'am,
The way to Arden Farm."

"That is my home," the
   white dog said;
"Good Farmer Austin's
   sheep
My father—Keeper is his
   name—
Is bound from thieves to
   keep."

"Then you're my cousin
    Blanche," said he.
"I'm Dash; in town well
    known;
A most distinguished lady's
    pet—
I scorn a vulgar bone!"

"Then I'm afraid, good
    cousin Dash,"
The white dog, laughing, said,
"That in our rural home
    you'll find
Yourself but poorly fed."

They walked together to the farm;
Blanche full of harmless glee,
And just outside the woodbine
    porch
Good old Keeper they did see.

Says Blanche, "This is our cousin
    Dash."
"He's welcome," Keeper said;
And into his snug dwelling-place
The town-bred dandy led;

And set before him rural fare:
Dash "did his best" to eat;
But in his secret heart he thought
Farm bacon quite a treat.

"You're come just in the nick o'
    time,"
The homely sheep dog cries;
While with fat bacon and good
    bones
He Dash's plate supplies.

"Tomorrow's the Hunt dinner,
    lad,
And they'll be glad to see
A friend of mine—a cousin too—
Rare fun it's sure to be.

"You hunt, no doubt?" "Sometimes," said Dash,
"A rat yields me some sport;
But hunting's out of fashion quite
With ladies in New York."

"Our ladies don't hunt now-a-days,"
Says Keeper; "that is true:
But what a New York lady says
Is naught to me or you."

Dash smiled and said, since he was there
He on a horse would mount;
As they were his relations true
He'd make a humble hound.

The next day, dressed out in their best,
To the Hunt feast they go;
And Keeper introduces Dash
To all he chanced to know.

The hounds had spread a jovial feast:
But I'm ashamed to say
How very foolishly poor Dash
Behaved upon that day.

He sniffed the soup; turned up his nose;
Asked every dish's name;
And sighing, said, "He hoped to make
His dinner upon game!"

Declared he only claret drank,
While all good home-brew quaffed;
Till at his airs and graces all
The honest fox-hounds laughed.

They offered him a mount next day;
And such was Dash's pride,
That he accepted it, although
He knew he couldn't ride.

So next day, on a fine gray steed,
He joined the merry Meet,
In top boots, spurs, and jacket "pink"—
A huntsman's garb complete.

Full soon the fox is found: they start;
Dash holds on by the mane;
His hat flies off—but he sticks on
Until a brook they gain.

"I wish I were a spaniel now!"
Cries Dash, in sore distress;
"I cannot swim in boots and spurs!
Oh, here's a pretty mess."

Pride had a fall, and Dash a spill;
He tumbled in the stream;
And as, indeed, he could not swim,
His peril was extreme.

By petting he's been
    spoiled outright:
He's only fit to stay
With some fine lady, in
    her room
To jump about and play."

"That's true," said
    Blanche; "yet this I
    know
Of my poor town-bred
    friend—
With his own feeble life,
    Dash would
His mistress kind defend.

A Newfoundland—at whom he's laughed
Because mere ale he drank—
Leaped down at once into the brook,
And drew him to the bank.

Weary and wet, he leads him home;
Dash vows he'll hunt no more.
They find his pretty cousin Blanche
Spinning beside the door.

"He's a good house dog; vain, I grant,
As puppies still will be;
This ducking will have done him good
As bye-and-bye you'll see.

"I dare say, if we went to town,
We might as awkward seem,
And find the streets as hard to cross
As Dash did our small stream."

Quite vexed to see her
    cousin's plight,
She made him go to
    bed;
And many a grateful
    word of thanks
She to the great dog
    said.

Smiling, he answered,
    "Pretty Blanche,
Send this poor puppy
    home;
It does not do for
    such as he
About the world to
    roam.

Blanche nursed Dash well, and he went back
To town, much wiser grown;
But of his further history
No more to us is known.

'Twas the Night before Christmas

'Twas the night before
  Christmas, when all
  through the house
Not a creature was
  stirring, not even
  a mouse;
The stockings were
  hung by the
  chimney with care,
In hopes that St
  Nicholas soon
  would be there.

The children were nestled all snug in their beds,
While visions of sugar-plums danced in their heads;
And Mamma in her kerchief and I in my cap,
Had just settled our brains for a long winter's nap—

When out on the lawn there rose such a clatter,
I sprang from my bed to see what was the matter:
Away to the window I flew like a flash,
Tore open the shutters and threw up the sash.

The moon, on the breast of
the new-fallen snow,
Gave a luster of mid-day to
objects below:
When, what to my wonder-
ing eyes should appear,
But a miniature sleigh, and
eight tiny reindeer;

With a little old driver, so
lively and quick,
I knew in a moment it must
be St Nick.
More rapid than eagles his
coursers they came,
And he whistled, and
shouted, and called them
by name—

"Now, Dasher! now, Dancer! now, Prancer and Vixen!
On! Comet, on! Cupid, on! Donder and Blitzen;

To the top of the porch, to the top of the wall!
Now, dash away, dash away, dash away all!"

251

As I drew in my head,
And was turning around,
Down the chimney St
    Nicholas
Came with a bound.

He was dressed all in fur
From his head to his foot
And his clothes were all
    tarnished
With ashes and soot:

A bundle of toys
He had flung on his back,
And he looked like a
    peddler
Just opening his pack;

His eyes how they twinkled!
His dimples how merry!
His cheeks were like roses,
His nose like a cherry;

His droll little mouth
Was drawn up like a bow,
And the beard on his chin
Was as white as the snow!

As dry leaves that before
The wild hurricane fly,
When they meet with an
    obstacle,
Mount to the sky;

So, up to the house-top
The coursers they flew,
With a sleigh full of toys—
And St Nicholas too.

And then in a twinkling
I heard on the roof
The prancing and pawing
Of each little hoof;

The stump of a pipe
He held tight in his teeth,
And the smoke, it encircled
His head like a wreath.

He had a broad face,
And a little round belly,
That shook when he
    laughed,
Like a bowl-full of jelly.

He was chubby and plump,
    a right jolly old elf;
And I laughed when I saw
    him in spite of myself.

A wink of his eye, and a twist of his head,
Soon gave me to know I had nothing to dread.

He spoke not a word, but went straight to his work,
And filled all the stockings, then turned with a jerk,
And laying his finger aside of his nose,
And giving a nod, up the chimney he rose.

He sprang to his sleigh, to his team gave a whistle,
And away they all flew, like the down of a thistle:
But I heard him exclaim 'ere he drove out of sight,
"Happy Christmas to all, and to all a good night!"

The Trial of the Sparrow Who Killed Cock Robin

This is the portrait of
Mr Cock Sparrow,
Who shot Robin
Redbreast with his
bow and arrow.
The Cuckoo was
ordered a strict search
to make
And bring him to justice,
his trial to take.

After poor Cock Robin was
laid in his grave,
And the birds had sung
round it a mournful stave,
They all of them went in
chase of the Sparrow,
Who had killed their friend
with his bow and arrow.

The Judge and the Jury
being solemnly met,
And the Court of Justice in
due order set,
Said the Judge to the Jury,
"Pray now beware:
A bird's life at stake is a
serious affair."

Then said Justice Hawk, "Though his crime rouses fury,
The rogue shall have justice from Judge and from Jury."
And then came the Cuckoo, who made a great din
As he dragged by the head the accused Sparrow in.

"When we found him, my Lord, he was stealing some grain—
The sparrows by thieving their livelihood gain,"
Said the Sparrow, "'Tis false! both I and my wife
Are honest as ever you were in your life.

"A few grains of wheat lay beside the barn door,
I picked them all up, and I did nothing more."
Said Jenny, "It is not for that we are here;
For killing my love at this bar you appear."

Said the Pig, "I was hastily called from my stye,
But came just too late to see Cock Robin die;
When asked by the Dog if I thought he was dead—
'Yes, quite dead and cold,' with great sorrow I said."

Said Puss, "I'm a doctor, so
   mind what I say;
I happened to pass on the
   very same day,
I saw the poor Robin the
   Sparrow had slain—
He was quite dead and cold,
   and would ne'er fly again."

Said the Dog, "I ran out of
   my kennel adjacent,
Or I think Dr Puss would
   have worried the patient;
However, Cock Robin was
   dead, I believe,
And that is the cause that we
   all of us grieve."

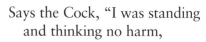

Says the Cock, "I was standing
   and thinking no harm,
When I saw Robin wounded,
   but could not tell where;
We put on our spectacles, those
   who had any,
And found that his wounds
   were both grievous and
   many."

Says the Hawk, "Since you are
   such a murdering elf,
I think I shall kill you and eat
   you myself."
So he ate up the Sparrow; the
   rest flew away:
They thought it not safe near
   such justice to stay.

Tit, Tiny and Tittens

The Greedy Kitten

Oh! Why do you nibble away at the cake?
'Twas never intended for kitten to take.
"Beware," cried the cat,
"How you meddle with that,
So scamper, scamper, scamper away."

Then Tiny obeyed her old mother the cat,
But Tittens, the rogue, was too greedy for
    that;
He liked the sweet crumbs,
With the raisins and plums,
So nibbled, nibbled, nibbled away!

But, oh! Was he not in a terrible fright,
When Susan, the kitchen-maid, came with
    a light!
And did not he wish
He'd ne'er tasted the dish,
When chased, chased, chased away!

The Cross Kitten

Tiny and Tittens were two little kittens,
As soft and white as the snow,
Who went to play, on a bright summer day,
Where ripe red cherries do grow.

The play was begun in mirth and in fun,
But Tittens soon tired of that;
The cross young rover knocked Tiny over,
And snarled like a tiger-cat.

How naughty was this, with a groan and a
    hiss
To spoil so happy a play!
With kittens or boys, 'tis temper destroys,
And takes all pleasure away.

The Disappointed Kitten

"Off! off!" cried the lady,
"Off, off, and away!
Go search the house for rat or mouse,
My bird shall not be your prey!

"I heard a sudden fluttering,
I heard a sudden fall;
For little Tit's bound had knocked to the
    ground
Flowerpot, flower, and all!

"I flew to save my darling,
The dreaded foe in view—
Oh! never fear, my birdie dear,
No kitten shall dine upon you!

"Off! off!" cried the lady,
"Off, off, and away!
Go search the house for rat or mouse,
My bird shall not be your prey!"

The Foolish Kitten

Oh! Tittens, he fancied to dine off the fish
That floated about in their elegant dish,
And often he eyed with a covetous wish
The prettiest one in the water—
All skimming, swimming, sliding, gliding,
Little fins her movement guiding,
Upwards now, then downwards riding—
Oh! if he could but have caught her!

So Tittens, one day, tried to catch at a fin,
When suddenly kitten went floundering in,
All struggling and kicking, and drenched to
    the skin,
His head and shoulders right over!
Tail lashing, splashing, soaking, choking,
Was ever accident so provoking!
Till his mistress, laughing, joking,
Pulled out the poor little rover!

The Merry Kitten

Tittens growled over a ducking he'd had;
Tit he complained that the weather was bad;
Up started Tiny with, "Never be sad;
Let's have a see-saw together,
Together how merry we'll be!

"You in your corner, all shivering and wet,
The longer you stay there the more you will
　　fret:
Jumping will warm you and make you
　　forget;
Let's have a see-saw together,
Together how merry we'll be!

"Tit, though the shower may heavily fall,
We can be happy in spite of it all,"
Tittens and Tit they sprang up at the call,
Gayly they gamboled together,
As merry as merry could be.

The Frightened Kittens

"Dear! oh, dear! a dog is near!"
Cried Tittens, ready to die with fear;
"One scratch of his claw, one gripe of his
　　paw,
Would finish us off in a minute!"
Then Tit he trembled, and Tiny too,
As if a lion had come in view,
When a mastiff tall entered the hall,
And looked around like the lord of all.
"Oh! will not he bite?" cried she—
"Oh! will not he fight?" cried he.
"If fight must be," said Tiny, "we
Will not be the first to begin it!"
But the noble mastiff, brave and strong,
Would not do a feeble kitten wrong.
'Tis cowards that seek to hurt the weak;
He would not have worried a linnet!

Lily Sweetbriar's Birthday

I have known many
  dear little people,
And numerous the
  charms they
  possessed;
But bright little Lily
  Sweetbriar
I ever loved dearest
  and best.

A child full of frolic and
  sunshine,
A wee, winsome,
  mischievous elf;
Yet gentle, and loving,
  and kindly,
She thought very little
  of self.

She came when the
  snowdrops were
  nodding
Over violets timid
  and sweet;
When pert little crocus
  looked daring,
And laughed at the
  cold driving sleet.

Dear reader, you've oft seen a sunbeam
Glide into a dark, dingy room,
And spread light and warmth by its presence,
Where all had been chillness and gloom.

Thus a child with a bright cheerful spirit
Sheds pleasure and gladness around,
In the home of the peer or the peasant,
Wherever its light may be found.

Papa was quite proud of his Lily;
And when her next birthday drew near,
Told Mamma to invite a large party,
For music, and games, and good cheer.

Lily's eyes shone like two little planets
When she heard the resolve of Papa,
And off to the nursery she scampered,
To relate the consent of Mamma.

260

Papa then produced a neat
  inkstand,
Mamma brought a golden-
  nibbed pen;
Lily sat down to write invitations,
"Tea at six, and the supper at ten."

At last dawned the longed-for
  morning,
And Lily woke up in delight;
The first thing that entered her
  wise head
Was, "My birthday, and party
  tonight."

The first to arrive was Aunt Susan,
Pale, pensive, and quiet, and fair;
She brought a pearl locket for Lily;
Inside was a piece of her hair.

And while she bestowed it, dear Auntie
Breathed over her darling a prayer,
"The Pearl of Great Price might be Lily's,
To keep her soul spotless and fair."

The next was Aunt Florence, the widow,
So calm and so sweetly resigned;
To know her was surely to love her,
So cheerful, so thoughtful, so kind.

A warm kiss she gave to dear Lily,
With a book bound in crimson and gold,
And murmured a prayer that her darling
Might stay good when young and when old.

And then Cousin Hector, the soldier,
All bombast, moustachios, and scent,
With a speech wherein nonsense abounded,
Presented a watch made by Dent.

And young Cousin Emma, the orphan,
Gave a purse made of blue silk and beads,
With a hope its contents might be always
Spent on kindly and generous deeds.

Next, pale Cousin
    Edward, the poet,
Brought a rose and a
    most melting lay,
Written all about
    Truth, Love, and
    Beauty;
Just fit for the child
    and the day.

Now, brave Cousin Hal, the young sailor,
Just returned from the perilous sea,
Had before jotted down in his log-book,
"Cousin Lily" and "Music and tea".

He brought two green birds from Australia,
A curious box from Japan,
A strange little idol from China,
And a lovely carved ivory fan.

On Bachelor Ben, the rich
  Uncle,
Red and portly, and brim-full
  of fun,
Every face in the room beamed
  a welcome;
Mamma said, "So glad that
  you've come!"

After answering all the kind
  greetings,
He held up his arm in the air,
And begged those who were
  present to notice
That not one sleeve-button
  was there!

Then he called aloud for niece Lily,
And declared he'd his darling disown
If she did not the very next minute
Sew the buttons, now wanting, all on.

"Oh, Uncle," said poor little Lily,
"You can't be in earnest, I know!
'Tis my birthday; I haven't my work-box;
You surely don't want me to sew?"

"Come hither, you pert little monkey,"
He said, with a shake of his head,
And drew out a beautiful housewife,
Full of buttons, and needles, and thread.

Poor Lily could hardly help crying;
But she knew that she must not be rude,
So at once did her best, by complying
With her Uncle Ben's whimsical mood.

Hal's blue eyes then opened still wider—
He thought her a fairy outright;
But I think both the soldier and poet
Were a "leetle bit" shocked at the sight.

Uncle Ben gave her cheek a
  sly pinching,
And then a good warm
  hearty kiss;
And Lily's sweet smile gave
  assurance
His joke was not taken amiss.

At last Uncle John, the
  young curate,
Came in, looking pale and
  careworn;
He had worked for the
  service of others
Till eve from the earliest
  morn.

And now he had come from
  a night-school;
It has once been a mere
  robbers' den;
Where he tried hard to
  turn boyish vagrants
Into honest and hard-
  working men.

He said he need not, for late coming,
Apology make, he well knew;
Then smilingly, from his coat-pocket,
A purple-bound volume he drew.

He said, with a look at dear Lily,
"Don't fear, I am not going to preach;
My gift if you ponder it duly,
Your duty, my darling, will teach.

"Take this book, my dear girl, for your
   guide,
Companion, and counselor sweet;
May its honey still sweeten your life,
Its lamp be a light to your feet.

"Drink often at Wisdom's pure fountain;
Weigh all in her balance of gold;
She has rubies and treasures to give you,
Whose value has never been told.

"Seek her early and she will be with you,
Imparting a beauty divine;
For they only who walk in her footsteps,
In true and pure loveliness shine."

Now came supper, and afterwards
   parting,
Warm wraps, and looks out at the sky;
Little laughs, kisses sweet, and good wishes;
And then the last cab, and "goodbye".

The Old Woman and the Peddler

There was an old woman, as I've heard tell,
She went to market her eggs to sell;
She went to market, all on a market day,
And she fell asleep on the king's
    highway.

Along came a peddler, whose name
    was Stout,
And he cut her petticoats, all round about;
He cut her petticoats up to her knees,
And this little old woman began to freeze.

Now, when the old woman did first awake,
She began to shiver, and she began to shake;
She began to wonder, and she began to cry,
"Lauk-a-mercy on me, this can't be I!

"But if it be I, as I hope it be,
I've a little dog at home, and he'll
    know me;
If it be I, he'll wag his little tail,
And if it be not I, he'll bark, and
    he'll wail."

Home went the little woman,
    all in the dark,
Up got the little dog, and he
    began to bark;
He began to bark, and she
    began to cry,
"Lauk-a-mercy on me, this
    is none of I!"

Hickety, Pickety

Hickety, pickety, my black hen,
She lays good eggs for gentlemen;
Gentlemen come every day,
To see what my black hen doth lay.

Nonsense
Poems

✦

There was a Young Lady of Dorking,
Who bought a large bonnet for walking;
But its color and size,
So bedazzled her eyes,
That she very soon went back to Dorking.

There was an Old Person of Cheadle,
Was put in the stocks by the Beadle;
For stealing some pigs,
Some coats, and some wigs,
That horrible Person of Cheadle.

There was an Old Man
    of El Hums,
Who lived upon nothing
    but Crumbs;
Which he picked off the
    ground,
With the other birds round,
In the roads and the lanes
    of El Hums.

There was an Old Man
    of the West,
Who never could get
    any rest;
So they set him to spin,
On his nose and his chin,
Which cured that Old
    Man of the West.

There was an Old Man of the Nile,
Who sharpened his nails with a file;
Till he cut off his thumbs,
And said calmly, "This comes
Of sharpening one's nails with a file!"

There was an Old Man
    who said, "How
Shall I flee from this
    horrible Cow?
I will sit on this stile,
And continue to smile,
Which may soften the
    heart of that Cow."

There was an Old Person of Hurst,
Who drank when he was not athirst;
When they said, "You'll grow fatter!"
He answered, "What matter?"
That globular Person of Hurst.

There was an Old Man of the coast,
Who placidly sat on a post;
But when it was cold,
He relinquished his hold,
And called for some hot buttered toast.

There was an Old Man
with a gong,
Who bumped at it all the
day long;
But they called out, "Oh
lor'!
You're a horrid old bore!"
So they smashed that
Old Man with a gong.

There was an Old Person
of Rheims,
Who was troubled with
horrible dreams;
So to keep him awake,
They fed him with cake,
Which amused that Old
Person of Rheims.

There was an Old Man
of Peru,
Who watched his wife
making a stew;
But once, by mistake,
In a stove she did bake
That unfortunate
Man of Peru.

There was an Old Man of
Madras,
Who rode on a cream-
colored Ass;
But the length of its ears,
So promoted his fears,
That it killed that Old
Man of Madras.

There was an Old Man
    of the West,
Who wore a pale
    plum-colored vest;
When they said, "Does it fit?"
He replied, "Not a bit!"
That uneasy Old Man of
    the West.

There was an Old Man of Corfu,
Who never knew what he should do;
So he rushed up and down,
Till the sun made him brown,
That bewildered Old Man of Corfu.

There was an Old Man
    who supposed,
That the street door was
    partially closed;
But some very large Rats,
Ate his coats and his hats,
While that futile Old
    Gentleman dozed.

There was an Old Person of Leeds,
Whose head was infested with beads;
She sat on a stool,
And ate gooseberry-fool,
Which agreed with that
Person of Leeds.

There was an Old Person of Cromer,
Who stood on one leg to read Homer;
When he found he grew stiff,
He jumped over the cliff,
Which concluded that Person of Cromer.

There was an Old Person of
Basing,
Whose presence of mind was
amazing;
He purchased a steed,
Which he rode at full speed,
And escaped from the
people of Basing.

There was an Old Man who said, "Well!
Will nobody answer this bell?
I've pulled day and night,
Till my hair has grown white,
But nobody answers this bell!"

There was an Old Man of
    Kilkenny,
Who never had more than
    a penny;
He spent all that money,
In onions and honey,
That wayward Old
    Man of Kilkenny.

There was an Old Person
    whose habits,
Induced him to feed upon
    Rabbits;
When he'd eaten eighteen,
He turned perfectly green,
Upon which he relinquished
    those habits.

There was an Old Man of
      the Cape,
Who possessed a large
      Barbary Ape;
Till the Ape, one dark night,
Set the house all alight,
Which burned that Old
      Man of the Cape.

There was an Old Man with a nose,
Who said, "If you choose to suppose,
That my nose is too long,
You are certainly wrong!"
That remarkable Man with
      a nose.

There was a Young Lady of Troy,
Whom several large Flies did annoy;
Some she killed with a thump,
      Some she drowned at the pump,
      And some she took with
            her to Troy.

There was an Old Man of Vienna,
Who lived upon Tincture of Senna;
When that did not agree,
He took Camomile Tea,
That nasty Old Man of Vienna.

There was an Old Person of Troy,
Whose drink was warm
brandy and soy;
Which he took with a spoon,
By the light of the moon,
In sight of the city of Troy.

There was an Old
Man in a pew,
Whose waistcoat was
spotted with blue;
But he tore it in
pieces,
To give to his Nieces,
That cheerful Old
Man in a pew.

There was an Old Person of Ems,
Who casually fell in the Thames;
And when he was found,
They said he was
    drowned,
That unlucky Old
    Person of Ems.

There was an Old Person of Buda,
Whose conduct grew ruder
    and ruder;
Till at last with a hammer,
They silenced his clamor,
By smashing that Person of Buda.

There was a Young Lady whose eyes,
Were unique as to color and size;
When she opened them wide,
People all turned aside,
And started away
    in surprise.

There was an Old Man
of Apulia,
  Whose conduct was
    very peculiar;
He fed twenty sons,
Upon nothing but buns,
  That whimsical Man of
    Apulia.

There was an Old Man of Kamschatka,
Who possessed a remarkably fat Cur;
His gait and his waddle,
Were held as a model
To all the fat
    dogs in
      Kamschatka.

There was a Young Person
  of Smyrna,
Whose Grandmother
    threatened to burn her;
But she seized on the Cat,
And said, "Granny, burn
    that!
You incongruous Old
  Woman of Smyrna!"

There was an Old Man
of Vesuvius,

Who studied the works
of Vitruvius;

When the flames burnt
his book,

To drinking he took,

That morbid
Old Man of
Vesuvius.

There was an Old Man
of th'Abruzzi,

So blind that he couldn't
his foot see;

When they said, "That's
your toe,"

He replied, "Is it so?"

That doubtful Old
Man of th'Abruzzi.

There was an Old Man
of the South,

Who had an immoderate
mouth;

But in swallowing a dish,

That was quite full of Fish,

He was choked, that Old
Man of the South.

There was an Old Man in a tree,
Who was horribly bored by
    a Bee;
When they said, "Does it buzz?"
He replied, "Yes, it does!
It's a regular brute of a Bee!"

There was a Young Lady of Wales,
Who caught a large Fish without scales;
When she lifted her hook,
She exclaimed, "Only look!"
        That ecstatic Young Lady
            of Wales.

There was a Young Lady of Clare,
Who was madly pursued by a Bear;
When she found she was tired,
She abruptly expired,
That unfortunate Lady
    of Clare.

There was an Old Lady of Chertsey,
Who made a remarkable curtsey;
She twirled round and
    round,
Till she sank underground,
Which distressed all the
    people of Chertsey.

There was an Old
    Person of Bangor,
Whose face was distorted
    with anger;
He tore off his boots,
And subsisted on roots,
That borascible Person of
    Bangor.

There was an Old Person of Tring,
Who embellished his nose with a ring;
He gazed at the moon,
Every evening in June,
That ecstatic Old Person of Tring.

There was an Old Man of the Dee,
Who was sadly annoyed by a Flea;
When he said, "I will scratch it!"
They gave him a hatchet,
Which grieved that Old Man of
 the Dee.

There was an Old Man with an Owl,
Who continued to bother and howl;
He sat on a rail,
And imbibed bitter ale,
Which refreshed that Old
 Man and his Owl.

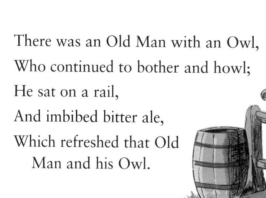

There was a Young Lady of Sweden,
Who went by the slow train to Weedon;
When they cried, "Weedon Station!"
She made no observation,
But thought she should go back to Sweden.

WEEDON STA.

There was an Old Man
of the Wrekin,

Whose shoes made a
horrible creaking;

But they said, "Tell us,
whether

Your shoes are of leather,

Or of what, you Old Man
of the Wrekin?"

There was an Old Man of Whitehaven,
Who danced a quadrille with a Raven;
But they said, "It's absurd,
To encourage this bird!"
So they smashed that Old
Man of Whitehaven.

There was an Old Man of
Messina,

Whose daughter was named
Opsibeena;

She wore a small Wig,

And rode out on a Pig,

To the perfect delight of
Messina.

There was a Young Lady of Russia,
Who screamed so that no-one could
    hush her;
Her screams were extreme—
No-one heard such a scream
As was screamed by that
    Lady of Russia.

There was an Old Person
    of Prague,
Who was suddenly seized with
    the plague;
But they gave him some butter,
Which caused him to mutter,
And cured that Old Person
    of Prague.

There was an Old Man with a poker,
Who painted his face with red ochre;
When they said, "You're a Guy!"
He made no reply,
But knocked them
    all down with
    his poker.

There was an Old Person of Gretna,
Who rushed down the crater of Etna;
When they said, "Is it hot?"
He replied, "No, it's not!"
That mendacious Old
Person of Gretna.

There was an Old Man of Peru,
Who never knew what he should do;
So he tore off his hair,
And behaved like a bear,
That intrinsic Old Man of Peru.

There was a Young Person
of Janina,
Whose uncle was always
a-fanning her;
When he fanned off her
head,
She smiled sweetly and said,
"You propitious Old
Person of Janina!"

There was an Old Person
of Mold,

Who shrank from
sensations of cold;

So he purchased some
muffs,

Some furs, and some fluffs,

And wrapped himself well
from the cold.

There was an Old Man of Calcutta,

Who perpetually ate bread and
butter;

Till a great bit of muffin,

On which he was stuffin',

Choked that horrid Old Man
of Calcutta.

There was an Old Man of Columbia,

Who was thirsty, and called
out for some beer;

But they brought it
quite hot,

In a small copper pot,

Which disgusted that
Man of Columbia.

There was an Old Person of Ewell,
Who chiefly subsisted on gruel;
But to make it more nice,
He inserted some Mice,
Which refreshed that Old Person
    of Ewell.

There was a Young Lady of Portugal,
Whose ideas were excessively nautical;
She climbed up a tree,
To examine the sea,
But declared she would never
    leave Portugal.

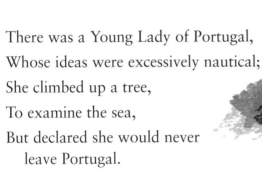

There was a Young Girl of Majorca,
Whose Aunt was a very fast walker;
She walked seventy miles,
And leaped fifteen stiles,
Which astonished that
    Girl of Majorca.

There was an Old Man
  with a beard,
Who sat on a
  Horse when he reared;
But they said, "Never mind!
You will fall off behind,
You propitious Old Man
  with a beard!"

There was an Old Person of Spain,
Who hated all trouble and pain;
So he sat on a chair with his feet in the air,
That umbrageous Old Person of Spain.

There was an Old Man in a boat,
Who said, "I'm afloat! I'm afloat!"
When they said, "No, you ain't!"
He was ready to faint,
That unhappy Old Man
  in a boat.

There was an Old Man in a casement,
Who held up his hands in amazement;
When they said, "Sir, you'll fall!"
He replied, "Not at all!"
That incipient Old Man
    in a casement.

There was an Old Man of Port Grigor,
Whose actions were noted for vigor;
He stood on his head,
Till his waistcoat turned red,
    That eclectic Old Man of
        Port Grigor.

There was a Young Lady of Ryde,
Whose shoe-strings were seldom untied;
She purchased some clogs,
And some small spotty Dogs,
And frequently walked about Ryde.

There was an Old Man of
the Hague,
Whose ideas were
excessively vague;
He built a balloon
To examine the moon,
That deluded Old Man of
the Hague.

There was an Old Person of Philœ,
Whose conduct was scroobious and wily;
He rushed up a Palm,
When the weather was calm,
And observed all the ruins
of Philœ.

There was an Old Person of Cadiz,
Who was always polite to all ladies;
But in handing his daughter,
He fell into the water,
Which drowned that
Old Person
of Cadiz.

There was an Old Man of the Isles,
Whose face was pervaded with smiles;
He sang "High dum diddle,"
And played on the fiddle,
That amiable Man of the Isles.

There was an Old Man
of Marseilles,
Whose daughters wore
bottle-green veils;
They caught several Fish,
Which they put in a dish,
And sent to their Pa at Marseilles.

There was an Old Person of Sparta,
Who had twenty-five sons and one "darter";
He fed them on Snails,
And weighed them
in scales,
That wonderful Person
of Sparta.

291

There was an Old Man
    of Dundee,
Who frequented the top
    of a tree;
When disturbed by the Crows,
He abruptly arose,
And exclaimed, "I'll return to Dundee!"

There was an Old Man of Leghorn,
The smallest that ever was born;
But quickly snapt up, he
Was once by a Puppy,
Who devoured that Old Man
    of Leghorn.

There was an Old Person of Chester,
Whom several small children did pester;
They threw some large stones,
Which broke most of his bones,
And displeased
    that Old
    Person of
    Chester.

There was a Young Lady of Poole,
Whose soup was excessively cool;
So she put it to boil,
By the aid of some oil,
That ingenious Young Lady
of Poole.

There was an Old Person of Nice,
Whose associates were usually Geese;
They walked out together,
In all sorts of weather,
That affable
Person of Nice!

There was a Young
Lady of Hull,
Who was chased by a
virulent Bull;
But she seized on a spade,
And called out, "Who's
afraid!"
Which distracted that
virulent Bull.

There was an Old Man who said,
   "Hush!
      I perceive a young bird
         in this bush!"
      When they said, "Is it small?"
      He replied, "Not at all!
      It is four times as big as the bush!"

There was a Young Lady of Turkey,
Who wept when the weather was murky;
When the day turned out fine,
She ceased to repine,
That capricious Young
   Lady of Turkey.

There was an Old Man on whose nose,
Most birds of the air could repose;
But they all flew away,
At the closing of day,
Which relieved that Old Man and his nose.

There was an Old Person of
    Rimini,
  Who said, "Gracious! Goodness!
    O Gimini!"
When they said, "Please be still!"
She ran down a Hill,
    And was never more heard of at
    Rimini.

There was an Old Man of
  the East,
Who gave all his children
  a feast;
But they all ate so much,
And their conduct was such,
That it killed the Old Man
  of the East.

There was an Old Man
  of the North,
    Who fell into a
      basin of broth;
  But a laudable Cook
  Fished him out with
    a hook,
  Which saved that Old Man
    of the North.

There was a Young Lady of Lucca,
Whose lovers completely forsook her;
She ran up a tree,
And said "Fiddle-de-dee!"
Which embarrassed the people of Lucca.

There was an Old Man of Cape Horn,
Who wished he had never been born;
So he sat on a chair
Till he died of despair,
That dolorous Old Man of Cape Horn.

There was an Old Person of Burton,
Whose answers were rather uncertain;
When they said, "How d'ye do?"
He replied "Who are you?"
That distressing Old Person of Burton.

There was an Old Person of Ischia,
Whose conduct grew friskier and friskier;
He danced hornpipes and jigs,
And ate thousands of figs,
That lively Old Person of Ischia.

There was an Old Man of Quebec—
A beetle ran over his neck;
But he cried, "With a needle,
I'll slay you, O beadle!"
That angry Old Man of Quebec.

There was an Old Person of Dover,
Who rushed through a
    field of blue clover;
But some very large Bees
Stung his nose and
    his knees,
So he very soon went
    back to Dover.

Acknowledgments

TEXT

Many nursery rhymes, verses and stories cannot be attributed to an author. We acknowledge below the rhymes, verses and stories whose authorship we were able to ascertain.

Kate Greenaway:
Ball
Bonny Johnny
Cross Patch
Little Tommy Tittlemouse
Miss Molly and the Little
    Fishes
On the Bridge
On the Wall Top
Susan Blue
The Tea Party
To London
To Mystery Land
Wishes

Edward Lear:
Nonsense Poems
Twenty-Six Nonsense
    Rhymes and Pictures

Alice Mills:
At the Table
Baby's Laughing Eyes
I Can be Anything
I Wish Today were
    Yesterday
Picking Flowers
Sleepy Harry
Umbrellas
We Love our Cat

Clement C. Moore:
'Twas the Night Before
    Christmas

ILLUSTRATIONS

Kate Greenaway:
pages 3, 152–160, 204–211,
    234–241, 298 (top), 304
    (top)

Wendy de Paauw:
pages 161–178, 298

Richard Doyle:
pages 138–151

Edward Lear:
pages 6 (top), 194–203,
    268–297, 304 (bottom)

John Tenniel:
pages 7 (top), 110–125

*Lialia and Valentin
    Varetsa:*
pages 7 (bottom), 88–108

Text Sources

Carroll, Lewis (1889). *The Nursery "Alice"*. London: Macmillan and Co.

Lang, Andrew (ed.) (1889). *The Blue Fairy Book*. London: Longmans, Green and Co.

Lang, Andrew (no date). *The Princess Nobody: A Tale of Fairy Land*. London: Longmans, Green and Co.

Paull, H. B. (translator). *Grimm's Fairy Tales*. London: Frederick Warne and Co.

Robinson Crusoe. Based on the stories by Daniel Defoe.

Index of First Lines in Nursery Rhymes

General Index

300

302

Publisher	Gordon Cheers
Associate publisher	Margaret Olds
Art director	Stan Lamond
Project manager	Marie-Louise Taylor
Cover design	Stan Lamond
Proofreading	Loretta Barnard
Production	Bernard Roberts
Foreign rights	Dee Rogers

This 2004 edition is published by Gramercy Books, an imprint of Random House Value Publishing, a division of Random House, Inc., New York, by arrangement with Global Book Publishing Pty. Ltd.

Gramercy is a registered trademark and the colophon is a trademark of Random House, Inc.

Random House
New York • Toronto • London • Sydney • Auckland
www.randomhouse.com

Printed and bound in China

A catalog record for this title is available from the Library of Congress.

ISBN 0-517-22395-3

10 9 8 7 6 5 4 3 2 1

Produced by Global Book Publishing Pty Ltd
1/181 High Street, Willoughby, NSW Australia 2068
tel 61 2 9967 3100 fax 61 2 9967 5891
First published in 2004